THUNDER
ON THE
DOS GATOS

Stallions at Burnt Rock
Long Road to LaRosa
The Stranger from Medina

WEST ★ TEXAS
SUNRISE

THUNDER
ON THE
DOS GATOS

A Novel

PAUL BAGDON

Fleming H. Revell
A Division of Baker Book House Co
Grand Rapids, Michigan 49516

© 2003 by Paul Bagdon

Published by Fleming H. Revell
a division of Baker Book House Company
P.O. Box 6287, Grand Rapids, MI 49516-6287
www.bakerbooks.com

Printed in the United States of America

Library of Congress Cataloging-in-Publication Data
Bagdon, Paul.
    Thunder on the Dos Gatos : a novel / Paul Bagdon.
        p.   cm. — (West Texas sunrise)
    ISBN 0-8007-5834-X
    1. Texas, West—Fiction. 2. Ranch life—Fiction. I. Title. II. Series.
PS3602.A39T47 2003
813'.54—dc21   2003007261

This novel is for my partner, Linda Toole—just as all the rest of them have been, and the future ones will be.

Prologue

The wood and steel bridge over the Dos Gatos River about twenty-five miles from Burnt Rock, Texas, should have lasted far longer than it did. With good periodic maintenance and no major catastrophes such as floods, hurricanes, lightning, or arson-generated fires, it may have lived long enough to celebrate its seventy-fifth or even one-hundredth birthday. It didn't, however—the bridge went down on April 15, 1881.

The West Texas Rail Road's scouts had determined that the lazy little burg of Burnt Rock was ideally located to handle huge numbers of beef, if only there was a bridge over the Dos Gatos. The town was already established as a farming community, and the main street of Burnt Rock was growing rapidly. There was a large mercantile, a blacksmith and livery operation, a café, a feed mill, and, unfortunately, a saloon, where gambling and drunkenness were not only permitted but encouraged. There was also a U.S. marshall's office occupied by lawman Ben Flood, who began his tenure a few years after the surrender of the Confederacy at Appomattox.

Silas Legg, a surveyor, architect, and builder in Burnt Rock, was awarded the contracts for the railroad depot and station in town and the elaborate maze of fences and gates of the stockyard. He also was selected to build the bridge over the Dos Gatos. It was agreed around town that Silas was as crooked as he was incompetent, and that he'd purchased the tremendously lucrative contracts from a dishonest crony in the employ of the railroad.

The laborers were confused, non-English-speaking Chinese men supplied by unscrupulous contractors—both white and Chinese. The workers were paid $1.20 per week, for six-and-a-half ten- to twelve-hour days. A percentage of the laborers' pay was tendered in scrip created by Silas Legg, scrip that could be used only at the store Legg and the labor contractors established near the bridge site.

Silas Legg, it must be admitted, knew his larcenous trade well. He buttressed cheap, inferior materials with good, standard-grade supplies where it was absolutely necessary to keep the structure standing.

The real wonder of the bridge over the Dos Gatos is that it remained standing for the eleven months that it did.

1

Lee Morgan's days always started early. The merest speck of light in the east set off the three roosters of Maria, wife of her ranch manager, Carlos, and the brood-mares and other horses housed in stalls overnight began snorting for feed as soon as the birds greeted the day. The horses in the pastures began drifting toward the gates of the fences, impatiently awaiting the sweet hay that soon would be forked from a flatbed by sleepy-eyed ranch hands.

This morning, the scent of smoked ham, fried potatoes, and chicory coffee wafted from Maria's kitchen. The crew wandered in to breakfast, scratching themselves, rubbing their eyes, yawning, or quietly discussing the day's work.

Lee stood next to Maria as Maria filled the plates and mugs of the ranch hands. They filed past her, their sleepiness washed away by the savory fragrance of the meal, and then headed outside with their plates. During the winter and through any spells of bad weather, the men ate in shifts in the kitchen, but on this fine early summer day, they preferred to breakfast outside, sitting on the ground in small groups.

"I'm going to ride over to the back pasture this morning," Lee said. "I want to check the fences and see if those geldings Carlos put out there are getting along—and make sure the mares are okay too."

"You'll ride Sleek, no? Ees funny how you always find a job that puts you on the back of that horse," Maria said.

"Slick's the finest stallion in Texas," Lee answered with a grin. "He needs a little exercise once in a while."

Maria snorted. "Horses, horses, horses. Thass all I hear round here. Horses, they're as bright as cheekens—an' a whole lot more trouble."

"Hard to saddle one of your roosters, though. And those chickens give out after half a day's work. How about this: When Carlos comes back from La Quatro with our new stallion, we'll put him to training chickens for range work, okay?"

"Carlos ees as loco about horses as you, Lee. Two days he ees gone to pick up thees new one, an' then he'll spend all his time with it, no? Don' you an' him know I need my husband round to keep me warm at night?"

Maria put her hands on her hips and tried to look stern, but in a moment, both women were laughing.

The main barn was still cool and night-humid, although the sun was beginning to manifest its early summer strength. The horses in the stalls had their muzzles buried in the grain boxes solidly attached to the heavy boards of the stalls and were munching their crimped oats contentedly, occasionally shifting their hooves as they ate.

Lee stopped just inside the big barn, allowing her eyes to adjust to the dusky light. She breathed deeply of the aroma of spring hay, clean horses, and creosoted wood.

Slick's head popped out of a water bucket as Lee approached his stall. Rivulets of fresh water drained from his mouth as he nickered at her.

She worked the latch on the stallion's stall, stepped inside, and then stood quietly, simply looking at her horse.

Slick was tall—approaching seventeen hands—and his coat gleamed like polished coal. The long muscles of his legs were well-defined, and his chest was broad, deep, and hard. He was unlike most tall horses, who could appear rangy. The breadth of his rear quarters and chest gave him a solidity and grace rarely encountered in such a large animal. And his eyes—the purest black—crackled with quick intelligence.

Lee ran her hand the length of Slick's neck and used her index finger to dig gently at the slight hollow at the base of his ear, a particular source of delight to him. He grunted like a sow in warm mud.

Horses were Lee's business, and she knew more about them—selecting them, breeding them, riding them, and training them—than 99 percent of the men who made their livings from the backs of their mounts. Justin Morgan, the legendary horseman single-handedly responsible for beginning the Morgan horse breed, was an ancestor of hers, and she'd grown up on his grandson Noah's farm in Virginia after the deaths of her parents.

She'd learned everything her uncle Noah knew—and maybe even more. Her dream, her goal, was to develop the perfect ranch horse: a hardy, intelligent, sure-footed mount that could work the twelve- and fourteen-hour days required of a cowboy and his horse, and be ready for another day the next morning. Slick was Lee's foundation stallion at the Busted Thumb Horse Farm, and the best, brightest, and fastest horse she'd ever owned.

Lee saddled and bridled Slick and led him from his stall to the outdoors. The temperature had crept up during the twenty minutes she'd spent in the barn. She could tell the day was going to be a hot one.

Lee looked at the sky above her, a cerulean blue expanse unflawed by even a snippet of cloud. The air tasted thick with humidity, and she had barely mounted when tiny streams of sweat appeared on her forehead from under her Stetson. She cantered Slick along a path leading to the back pastures, waving to her ranch hands as she passed. Slick broke a healthy sweat before they were out of sight of the barn.

The prairie ahead of Lee appeared to spread out to forever. The pastures, fenced with smooth wire stretched between stout posts dug into the ground every fifty feet, seemed silly in their size, mere minuscule drops of water in an infinite ocean when contrasted with the open land beyond.

Soon the chambray shirt Lee was wearing stuck to her back like a sodden blanket. She tugged off her Stetson and wiped her forehead with a tattered bandana from the pocket of her culottes.

As she sat there for a moment, Ben Flood drifted into her mind. She could feel a smile spread over her face at the thought of him. She was sure of his love for her and sure of his integrity as a Christian and as a man. But the fact that he carried a gun and lived an often violent life frightened her. And she had difficulty reconciling his work as a lawman—a Texas marshall—with a Christian outlook. Still, she realized how important law was in the West, how the good and honest people needed a defender against the outlaws and drifters who rode in and out of towns, looking for nothing but easy and illegal profit and the satisfaction of their whiskey-thirst and salacious urges.

Lee was reining Slick toward a shallow pond where seven of her pregnant broodmares were clustered, cropping at the sweet grass near the shore, when she heard a scream.

She recognized the sound, a high-pitched, chilling squeal that no other animal could duplicate. It was a sound she rarely heard, but she knew the scream was a sure bet a horse was in trouble.

Lee whirled Slick toward a gentle rise that lay between them and the source of the sound. As Slick sprinted up the slope, a chestnut mare, heavy and ponderous with an almost-due foal, lumbered clumsily toward them. Her eyes were wide, and thick strands of spittle hung from between her gaping jaws. The foal within her shifted grotesquely from side to side as she ran, rippling her heaving, sweat-drenched sides.

Lee saw precisely what was going to happen, and there wasn't a thing she could do to stop it.

The panicked mare was running too hard to control her unbalanced body as she hurtled down the slope. A front leg folded under her, and her chest slammed into the earth with the force of a cannonball. The sharp crack of the mare's foreleg brought a helpless, anguished scream from Lee as she wheeled Slick toward the downed horse. Another mare topped the rise, this one a flashy pinto, also obviously pregnant and as unstable on her feet as the first. Her momentum and the force of gravity dragged her down into the dirt in a rolling, leg-flailing, frenzied heap.

A longhorn steer charged over the rise, its brindle body gleaming under a sheen of dripping sweat and plate-sized spatters of blood. Two twenty-yard strands of fencing wire and two fence poles churned a cloud of grit into the air behind the beast. One length of wire was tightly wrapped around a yard-long horn and between the steer's front legs, where a patch of flesh the size of a large man's hand had already been abraded away. The second line of fence wire was twisted into the first line, a Gordian knot of steel wire, cow flesh, weeds, and dirt.

Lee was standing thirty feet to the right of the heaving longhorn when the steer stopped, its front legs spread awkwardly, the twisted wire holding his massive head slightly to one side. The gruesome spectacle of the tortured animal clutched at Lee's heart like a fist, and she unconsciously raised her hand to her mouth.

The steer clumsily turned its body so that it faced Lee. Her eyes and those of the longhorn met for a half second of time. Never before had she experienced a more blatant manifestation of raw hatred.

The charge was a stumbling, lurching assault like that of a derailed but upright locomotive, with the fence wire hindering normal movement of the longhorn's front legs. Lee powered Slick into a wide arc that took her toward the chestnut. The mare was quiet now, but her sides continued to move jerkily with spasms of pain. Lee checked the position of the longhorn as she swung down from her saddle. He'd drifted farther away from her in his directionless charge and now stood, sides pumping as his immense lungs sucked air.

The mare sighed heavily, and the air rattled in her chest and put a faint red mist in the air at her muzzle. Then she lay still. Lee rushed to the animal's rear and wrenched her tail aside, but the amount of blood soak-

14

ing into the earth beneath the mare's haunches told her nothing could be done for the foal. It too was no doubt dead. Still, she had to try. If a spark of life still existed in the unborn creature, she wanted it to have its chance in the world.

Lee plunged her right arm deep into the mare's womb, her hand seeking out any motion, any indication of a beating heart. Slick snorted a challenge that conveyed as much fear as it did warning. Lee looked up. The steer was moving again, its ungainly attack now focused on the second fallen mare, the pinto. Lee closed her eyes, channeling all her senses into the fingertips within the dead mare.

She slowly removed her hand from the horse as tears slipped from her eyes. Slick danced in place, beginning to show more fear as the steer lumbered toward them. Lee stood and extended her arm to the rifle scabbard attached to the right side of her saddle. It was empty. And the Smith and Wesson .38 she sometimes carried during peak rattlesnake season was home in the nightstand next to her bed—unloaded and wrapped in a piece of oilcloth. But she knew the handgun would have no more effect than throwing clods of dirt at the longhorn anyway.

She swung into her saddle. Slick needed no prompting; he was in a full gallop within a few yards, stretching each of his muscles to put distance between himself and the juggernaut that had spread the acrid stink of blood, fear, and death over the pasture.

Lee formed a frantic, partially articulated prayer in her mind as Slick dug for home. She asked that the steer stay where he was, that his crazed charges not take him into the other pastures where other pregnant mares were grazing.

As she approached the ranch at top speed, she saw Maria hoeing in her garden. Then she heard the yell of Petey, one of the ranch hands. Maria snapped her head up from her work and looked at the open prairie around her.

Maria sprinted toward the emergency bell with skirts flying, her grace and speed belying her age and size. She yanked the handle powerfully, and the first notes pealed out over the prairie.

Two men ran out from the main barn, one clutching a lever-action 30.30 from the weapons closet maintained there. A nearby ranch hand skidded his Appaloosa to a sliding stop near Maria, and another man bolted from the breeding barn cradling a shotgun. Lee barreled toward them, yelling, "Rifles! Bring rifles!" She jammed Slick to a stop and reached toward the cowboy with the 30.30. He tossed it to her, and she grabbed it out of the air as she turned Slick. "Follow me!"

She couldn't run Slick back to the pasture as she had coming in. She held him to a lope and listened carefully to his breathing over the hollow thud of his hooves on the soil. He showed no signs of weakening, although he was sweating heavily.

The noise of the horses running behind her was a welcome sound. The seven men now clustered behind Slick drew up closer to her and spread out, letting her continue to ride point. When she reined in and worked the lever of the rifle, they rode up to her, forming a ragged line.

The steer charged the closest horseman; the fractured fence posts still clattered behind the beast, as if urging him on to more blood and death. The rifle volley lasted perhaps twenty seconds, but it seemed to be a block of frozen time to Lee—an unending fusillade of heavy-caliber bullets that rendered the longhorn just as dead as the mares and their unborn foals he had killed. After the steer lay still, she couldn't take her eyes from the animal.

"Miss Lee?" The familiar voice of a long-time ranch hand broke into her thoughts. "You okay? Your shirt's kinda bloody, ma'am."

Lee looked down in surprise. Dried blood was flaking from her arm and hand, and her chest was colored with it. "It's not my blood, Luke. I tried to see if I could birth one of the foals. I couldn't." She paused. "Get some of the boys out here to restring the fence and drag the steer back to the barn. Have somebody dress him out. We'll need a crew out here to bury the mares too."

"Yes'm." The cowboy began to turn his horse.

"Luke—two more things. Make sure anyone who rides any distance from the barn is armed with a rifle or shotgun. I won't watch this happen again."

"Sure, Miss Lee. I'll see to it."

"You want me to go after Marshall Flood?" another cowhand asked.

Lee shook her head. "No. The damage here is already done, and he has enough problems in town. He's coming for dinner tomorrow night, and I'll tell him then. Or maybe I'll send someone in the morning. I need to think on it." She turned back to Luke. "I'm going to put you in charge when Carlos and I aren't here. You're a good man. You deserve the promotion. I'll jack your pay fifteen a month too."

Luke's smile made his grizzled, weatherworn face glow. "Thankee, Miss Lee. The Busted Thumb's the best I ever worked for." He rode off quickly, as if he were hiding something. Lee suspected it was the hint of a blush she detected under the years of West Texas tan.

She turned to speak to the others. "I need to walk Slick out a bit. I'll be in before long. You men heard what I told Luke, didn't you?"

The riders nodded or mumbled that they had.

"Good. From now on, Luke speaks for me, just like Carlos does." She forced a smile. "Think anybody in Texas didn't hear our bell?"

"I'd wager Maria, she'll be hearin' it for a few more hours," a hand said with a grin. All the men chuckled, as if relieved by the break in the tension.

"Men," Lee added, "thanks."

She watched their backs as they rode off and then reined toward the dead longhorn. The animal seemed somehow smaller now, perhaps in the manner that a dead rattler seems to lose some of its length after it's been killed.

A flicker in the sky caught Lee's eye. A pair of buzzards scribed a long arc far over her; whatever brutish mechanism drew the carrion eaters to dead animals was already working. There'd be others soon. Lee wouldn't leave the area until the crew arrived.

She dismounted and walked away from Slick and closer to the steer. The stallion was trained to ground tie when she left him, and she had no more doubt that he'd stay put than she did the sun would rise in the east every morning. The longhorn's right flank was up as it lay sprawled in the dirt. The single, foot-long curving representation of a snake with a forked tongue was clear—the brand was that of the Long Snake Cattle Company.

Lee stepped into a stirrup and eased Slick ahead at a slow walk. He'd covered some ground for her, and she wanted to make sure he was properly cooled down. His breathing had long since returned to normal, and although his sides and chest were still damp, he was drying well.

The air, Lee noticed, still carried the metallic tang of gunpowder and blood. Carlos had warned her, and so had Ben, that it was foolish not to carry a rifle on her saddle and a handgun on her person. Still, that concept both angered and saddened her. Her life wasn't about guns and violence and battles. It was about the beauty of the land and the bond that existed between good horses and good people.

"This is the West," they'd told her. *"This is the far edge of civilization."* But she couldn't help but wonder if the hue of violence that colored the land would ever be altered if every man and woman carried weapons everywhere they went.

Two years ago she'd ridden into Burnt Rock to find Ben Flood facing a man who was standing fifty feet down the street. She'd lived in West Texas long enough to realize what was happening, and she darted Slick into an alley, out of the line of fire. Ben's back had been to her, and she couldn't see his face. The other man down the street had chiseled, craggy features and wore a poncho that ended in a sloppy fringe at his waist. His pistol was holstered low on his leg, just as Ben's was. His hands were at his sides, and his fingers were curled slightly inward, with his boots a foot and a half apart, the right one slightly forward. Ben's stance was almost a mirror image. She couldn't quite hear their words— the few words that were exchanged—but she saw the mouth of Ben's opponent move as he spoke. Finally, the man in the poncho spat onto the ground and turned away toward a horse tied in front of the Drovers' Inn. He mounted without another look at Ben and jogged his horse toward the end of Main Street.

19

Ben had watched the man leave town, and then walked to his office. Lee had waited until he'd shut the door before she rode out of the alley and back to the Busted Thumb. The stark similarity between the two men and the instruments of death that hung at their sides had chilled her at the moment and still brought shudders when she allowed the image into her mind.

She shivered and pushed the thought away. Turning her attention to Slick, she exerted some leg pressure. Slick responded immediately, as he always did. His muscles tightened under her as he extended his reach and increased his speed to a gentle, rocking-chair lope. She turned him to the left and began a wide figure eight. The precision with which Slick turned the eights calmed Lee, and the action on the ground kept the circling buzzards in the sky.

Soon Lee heard horses approaching and reined in. Moments later the clatter of a flatbed reached her. The wagon pulled next to the steer, and five men jumped down, grim-faced as they looked over the two mares. They took picks and shovels from the wagon and began walking toward the closest horse. Lee rode over to them.

"Nice and deep, please," Lee said. "These were fine animals."

"They was that, Miss Lee," one hand said. "I'm—all of us fellas—are right sorry for the loss."

A tall man dropped the pick he'd been carrying and took another couple of steps toward Lee. He was barely older than a boy, and she doubted that a razor needed to touch his face more than once a week, if that often. His eyes were a striking cornflower blue, but just now they glinted behind tears.

"Nothin' like this is gonna happen again round here, Miss Lee," he said. "We ain't gonna let it."

Lee nodded, speechless. She'd never seen a Western man cry before. She looked away from his face, and her gaze stopped at his waist. He was wearing an army Colt that was older than he was.

"Donny," Lee said. "You're armed. You know my rule about—"

"But Luke, he said you tol' him to tell us all . . ."

Lee shook her head. "I'm . . . yes, I did. It's okay—but just until this is all over. I . . . it's okay, Donny." She turned Slick away before her words became more befuddled.

As she rode off, the clink of the pickax against a rock reached her over the thudding of Slick's hooves. The sound made her shiver.

2

Ben could feel the vein at his right temple throbbing. His hands rested on his desk in front of him, but they were clenched together so powerfully that his knuckles had turned a pale white.

"Why didn't someone come for me right away? All the Busted Thumb hands know that if somethin' bad happens, they ride for me at a gallop."

"Miss Lee, she said not to, Marshall. She put Luke in charge, seein' that Carlos was off fetchin' up a new horse. She said—"

"Both mares dead, then, and the foals?" Ben interrupted.

"Yessir. An' the steer too. Like I said, it had a Long Snake brand on it." The young man paused and then swallowed hard. His voice rose to a high note and brought a blush to his face when it did so. "Marshall, I ain't been a hand at the Thumb but maybe two months. I didn't know any rule 'bout comin' right for you."

Ben exhaled audibly, fighting the hot blood that had risen as the cowhand told him about what had happened at the Busted Thumb the day before. "Okay, Billy, you didn't know."

"Uhh . . . it's Willy, Marshall. Willy Salzworthy."

"Willy. Right. Sorry. Look, let's make a deal between the two of us, okay? The next time anythin' like this happens, you saddle up and pound dirt for Burnt Rock an' me. I'll set things straight with Lee afterward. Even if you suspect you might be cryin' wolf, you come ahead at a gallop anyway. Are we clear on that?"

"I like my job at the Thumb a whole lot, Marshall. If you're real sure you can make things right with Miss Lee after I up an' ride off, I'll do just like you said."

Ben unclenched his hands. "You've got my word on that, Willy. It's like you're workin' for me, kinda undercover like some of the Pinkerton agents do. It's an important job."

The boy's eyes showed a rush of pride. "Like the fellas who was after the James an' Younger gang?" he asked.

"Exactly," Ben said. He reached across his desk to seal the deal with a handshake—but that was as far as he got. A piercing, feminine scream from the street put Ben in motion to the door of the office.

A young cowhand was writhing in the dirt of Main Street, clutching at the lower part of his leg. Blood was spewing scarlet on the dust. A longhorn, a thousand-pound bull with a span of almost five feet between the tips of his horns, wheeled about and gored the cowhand's horse again, sinking two feet of dagger-sharp horn into the downed animal's chest. So powerful was the red-eyed, enraged bull that he lifted the horse's body from the grit of the street and shook it like a terrier with a rat.

The cowboy, his face a flat, cadaverous gray, fumbled for his pistol as the bull slammed into the horse again. A woman standing at the door of Scott's Mercantile screamed. Bessie O'Keefe burst out of the café owned by her father and sprinted toward the marshall's office, yelling, "Ben! Ben! Quick!"

Ben stood outside his office for a moment, scanning the street. In another half second he spun on his heel and dashed back inside. When he ran out the second time, he was jacking a round into the chamber of a rifle.

His eye caught the opening of the door to the medical dispensary down the street, and he bellowed, "Doc— hold!" as he raised the 30.30 to his shoulder.

The bull was moving again, head low, the tips of his horns dripping with blood. Long strands of spittle were swinging from the corners of his mouth, and his crusted red eyes glinted insanely.

Ben fired twice. The longhorn's sweating, blood-streaked hulk collapsed to the street. The beast gouged a rut in the dirt with its momentum and then was still, its horn tips four feet from the now unconscious wrangler.

Doc, already at the downed man's side, yelled to the gawking lunch customers in O'Keefe's doorway, "Get this fellow to my office—now!"

Ben hustled up to Doc as a pair of men gently lifted the cowboy. "Anything I can do?" he asked.

Doc shook his head. When he spoke, his voice was tight and his words clipped. "I'll stop the bleeding and sew him up. He's not going to die, but I doubt that his right leg will be worth much for the rest of his life."

Ben nodded but didn't speak. Doc met his eyes. "I'll be the first one to ask a question you're going to hear until you're sick of it over the next few days, Ben. What was that creature doing in the middle of town? Suppose school had just gotten out? Suppose Missy Joplin or one of the older folks who can't move too sprightly had been on the street?"

"The bridge, Doc—the herds are buildin' up because of it. I'm gonna . . ."

But the physician was scurrying after the men carrying his patient. Ben figured it was no use speaking to the man's back, so he walked the couple of steps to where the dead bull lay and stood at its side. Flies were already settling on the animal. On its flank, clearly visible through sweat, mud, and streaks of blood, was the X2 brand. He turned away from the corpse and strode toward the livery stable.

It was cool inside the big barn, and the clean scent of good hay, well-groomed horses, and oiled leather greeted him as he walked over to Howard Angelo, the blacksmith and livery owner.

Howard was already pouring two large mugs full of coffee. He handed one mug to Ben. "Nice shot," he said.

Ben sipped at his coffee. "Like shootin' a barn, Howard—hard to miss."

"Whose stock?"

"X2. I'll be ridin' out there shortly. I told Shep Nelson to keep a close watch on his beef or move them on. I guess maybe he didn't listen to me."

"It's a long haul to the next cow town, Ben. The herds are rollin' in now, and those ramrods don't want to run no weight offa their beef. I took me a ride out to the stockyard yesterday. Easy-Bar has the corrals 'bout full. A couple of the wranglers told me they're runnin' low on feed."

26

"Yeah. I know." Ben shook his head. "The drives are gonna have to move on. There's no way round it. One of the Long Snake steers killed a couple of Lee's horses yesterday, and now this. I can't have longhorns runnin' in the streets, and with that many herds out there, the cowboys are gonna be itchy to spend their trail money. They'll tear up the town." He sighed. "The railroad will get the bridge back up as soon's they can, but it's still gonna be a few months."

Howard wiped sweat from his dark forehead with the back of his hand. "Gonna be trouble."

Ben swirled the coffee in his mug and then took a long drink from it. "Maybe," he said. "Look, Howard, I need a favor. Can you use your draft horses to haul the bull out of the middle of the street? If you care to butcher it up, you take all the beef you want an' give the rest to anybody who wants it. If you can find some men to dig, I'd appreciate your plantin' the cowboy's horse too." He reached into his vest pocket and pulled out a pair of silver dollars. "This oughta cover their work."

"I know just the boys," Howard said, taking the money. He was quiet for a moment. "This ain't gonna get no better, Ben. When I rode to the stock pens, I had some bad thoughts come back to me from when I was a sprout."

"What kinda thoughts?"

The blacksmith hesitated again. "Right frightenin' thoughts about all them longhorns."

"I didn't think there was anything that stood on four hooves that could scare you, Howard. What're you talkin' about?"

"You ever hear of St. Elmo's fire? Ever seen it?"

"I've heard of it. Never seen it, though. The balls of blue light that kind of roll around from point to point, right? Treetops and cactus and so forth?"

"Yeah, that's it. When I was a kid livin' in Kansas on my ma an' pa's spread, I saw it. I'll tell you this—I never seen such a spooky thing in my life, 'fore or since. My pa didn't have a big herd of longhorns—maybe three, four hundred. The St. Elmo's fire got to flamin' an' touchin' on the tips of the horns of those beef, and they just went crazy. They come over a grade from the pasture like Satan hisself was chasin' 'em, with those awful blue globs of light leapin' from one animal to another, an' there weren't nothin' that coulda stopped that stampede. About half the herd hit the barn, an' they just run right over it, Ben—like that stout ol' buildin' was made of paper or somethin'. Killed my pa's mules an' my own horse and my ma's little drivin' pony."

Ben was surprised to see tears spring from his friend's eyes.

"Killed my oldest brother too," the blacksmith went on. "An' a pal of his who was helpin' him put new rims on my ma's little two-seat, Sunday-go-to-church wagon." He drew a shuddering breath. "You seen what cannons shootin' chains an' scrap metal can do to a man's body in the war. Well, my brother and that other fella . . ." The blacksmith turned away.

Ben stepped forward and closed a hand over Howard's shoulder. "I'm sorry," he said quietly. "I didn't know about any of that."

The blacksmith dragged a sleeve across his face and turned back to Ben. "Ain't somethin' I like to talk about." He cleared his throat. "I'll take care of the horse an' bull, Ben."

"Good," Ben said. "Thanks for the help." He paused for a moment, finished his coffee, and set the mug on top of a stack of crimped-oat sacks. "Howard?"

The blacksmith looked up.

"Your coffee is still worse'n the swill I make."

Howard forced a grin, but in a heartbeat it turned real. "Ain't nothin' worse than your coffee, Marshall."

Snorty, Ben's horse, was half asleep in the sun in the enclosure behind the marshall's office. Ben walked into the one-stall outbuilding also within the enclosure and hefted Snorty's saddle, blanket, and bridle. He walked back out into the sun where his horse stood.

Snorty grunted through his nostrils as Ben tossed the blanket over the animal's back and smoothed it gently. He eased on the stock saddle that he'd paid far more for than a man of his meager finances should spend on a saddle. But Ben never regretted a penny of the price. The saddle fit Snorty's back perfectly—the Flathead Indian who'd handcrafted it with Ben's specifications had seen to that. The leather itself was from prime hides, without a blemish or range scar, and was redolent of the scent of carefully tanned and aged cowhide.

Ben fit the low port bit with the brass mouthpiece into the horse's mouth and slipped the bridle over Snorty's ears. An image of the cowboy's gored mount flashed in his mind. He reached out and stroked his own horse's neck. Snorty grunted with pleasure.

Ben jogged past the end of Main Street and headed for the stockyard a couple of miles outside of Burnt Rock. The smell of thousands of confined animals reached him before their constant, mournful bawling did. Six acres of cattle jammed into stout-fenced areas of a quarter-acre each spread before him as he topped a small rise. The fences, bleached by the unremitting sun, were intersected by eight-foot-wide chutes that led to the railroad tracks, where the longhorns would board cattle cars for their last ride.

Snorty moved nervously under Ben, confused by the scents of thousands of living things and the sound of shuffling hooves and the deep hum of restless cattle. Ben looked over at a cowboy who was using a pair of mules to drag the corpse of a gored cow toward a group of a dozen or so other dead animals a hundred yards away from the pens. Ben swung that way, unwrapping the latigo strip holding his canteen to his saddle horn.

"Hot work," he said, tossing the canteen to the cowhand. "My name's Ben Flood."

The wrangler grinned, showing all three of his yellow front teeth. "Ain't likely to get frostbit out here," he said. "I'm Hubbard Mott. Pleased ta meetcha." He pulled the cork from the canteen and drank greedily, water washing around his mouth and down his neck. "Thankee," he said, replacing the cork and tossing the canteen back. He eyed Ben's badge and added, "Marshall."

"Looks like your beef is gettin' feisty, Hubbard," Ben said, nodding toward the dead cow.

"I cain't say as I blame 'em. They don't have no more room than peas in a durn pod. Gettin' water to 'em ain't nothin' but impossible, an' tryin' to work 'em from horseback when they's this hot an' thirsty is like tryin' to herd a boxcar fulla sidewinders."

"Whose stock is here?"

"X2—I'm with them—an' Harp Master's Runnin' Nine."

Ben turned toward some hoarse shouting from the far side of the pens. "How're the boys gettin' along? If I recall, the Nines never had much use for the X2 crew."

"That's true enough. They been pretty much okay, though. Some dustups an' punch-outs, but not a real lot. Me, I don' git involved. I cain't see no sense in it. They been playin' some baseball, one drive against t'other.

30

The riders ain't got much to do. Some of 'em, they ride into Busted Rock to that there Drovers' Inn an' ride back out here in a day or two an' ain't fit to do no work for at least another day." He thought for a moment, his wrinkled face pensive. "It ain't what a man would call a Sunday school picnic, out here. Most of these riders, they ain't but a inch better'n the cattle they drive. I'm jist as happy to see 'em ride off to Busted Rock, truth be told."

"It's Burnt Rock, partner, not Busted Rock."

"Oh. Busted Rock's what I heard. I know there's a sign, but it's all shot up an' I couldn't read her." He paused for a moment. "Thing is, I haven't had no time to learn to read real good. No offense meant, Marshall."

"None taken," Ben said. "Seen anything of the Long Snake drive?"

"Not yet, but I hear they's on their way. Big herd, is what the boys are sayin'."

"How're the fences holding?"

"So far, okay. I'll tell you what, though—one good scare, an' these cattle are gonna stampede. You can feel it in the air—all them animals never had no fence around 'em nor another beef pressin' on 'em. If they up an' decide to head to your town, there ain't gonna be nothin' left for you to put back together."

The sharp crack of the stout bat against a rawhide-wrapped rock was so much like the report of a pistol that Ben's hand instinctively found the grips of his Colt as he swung Snorty in the sound's direction. The batter, a very tall and skinny man, was already halfway to first base, his long legs pumping high, his knees seeming to reach almost to his chin as he ran. The makeshift ball continued upward in a long, powerful arc. The first baseman took two steps toward the runner, planted his boots solidly, and delivered a roundhouse right-cross that dropped the lanky runner as if he'd slammed directly into a stone wall.

A man on the sidelines—a teammate of the now unconscious batter—drew a pistol and fired three quick shots at the first baseman. The pitcher hauled a long-barreled army Colt from his holster and pulled the trigger several times, but the beat-up and rusted weapon didn't fire. The third baseman, a Bowie knife grasped in his hand, ran toward the opposing team clustered around home plate. The second baseman had run in and was rolling in the dirt, punching, kicking, gouging, and cursing with the opposing catcher.

A short, fat wrangler with bandoliers of ammunition draped across his chest was attempting to wrestle a Winchester rifle from the saddle scabbard on his rearing, wide-eyed horse. A loud *thunk* sounded over the yelling and cursing, but this time the bat had struck the back of a head rather than the makeshift baseball.

Ben launched Snorty toward the brawling group, tugging his rifle free of its scabbard as he galloped toward the fight. Snorty charged through the main cluster of combatants, slamming into them like a battering ram, hurling men into the air and crashing others to the ground. Ben fired, and the report got everyone's attention.

"Cut it out, you bunch of lunatics!" Ben bellowed. "I'll arrest the whole pack of you if I have to!"

The grappling and punching stopped, and the men backed away from one another slowly, like a pack of timber wolves challenged by their alpha male. When a cowhand reached toward an unlabeled bottle of whiskey on the ground, Ben swung the barrel of his rifle seemingly without aiming and pulled the trigger again. The bottle disappeared in a cloud of grit and dirt that erupted from the ground, and a mist of acrid-smelling whiskey rose into the air.

"Where are your trail bosses?" Ben demanded. "Where's Shep Nelson?"

"In town, gettin' drunk," a cowboy with blood dripping from his lower lip answered. "They ain't got time to waste with no tinhorn lawman, would be my guess."

Ben locked eyes with the cowhand. A grin—more of a smirk, really—remained on the hand's face, but his eyes glistened like bits of polished coal. Ben stared into the fire, unflinching. The moment extended for an eternity.

The sharp crack of splintering wood gave the cowboy a chance to break the contest. A calf had pushed a bottom slat of fencing away and was hightailing it toward the open prairie. The cowboy looked away, and Ben's eyes followed his. A man riding a stout chestnut gelding galloped up to within ten feet of the calf and dropped a loop over it with casual ease.

Ben looked back at the cowboy. "I want you boys to make sure Nelson and the Nine's ramrod get my message: These cattle gotta be moved on. They got any problem with that, they come an' see me."

The smirk returned to the cowhand's face. "Nice talkin' to you, Marshall. I got work to do now." He turned away, heading to the pens. The baseball players followed him, several limping, a few with bloody noses, all with bruises on their faces. One cowboy yanked out a dangling tooth from between bloodied lips, inspected it for a moment, and then tossed it aside.

Snorty was happy to leave the strange smells and sounds behind as he carried Ben at a ground-eating lope across the desolate face of the prairie. Ordinarily, Ben would have enjoyed the ride and the solitude, but his meeting with the cattlemen troubled him. There were simply too many cattle jammed into too small a space, and the fact that the men who controlled the animals were as unpredictable as hawks added more danger to the mix.

Snorty smelled the water before Ben saw it—a wagon-bed-sized hole that had some water at the bottom. The tracks in the dirt around the clear water showed that the smaller denizens of the prairie depended on the pool. Coyotes, prairie chickens, roadrunners, prairie dogs, jackrabbits—all had left their prints behind after they'd assuaged their thirst.

Ben noticed that all the tracks veered sharply away from a cluster of brambles and buffalo grass adjacent to the pool. He understood why as he dismounted and led Snorty to the water. The ominous buzz that sounded like a handful of small pebbles being shaken in an empty tin can told him a diamondback lurked in the brush, awaiting a careless creature that would not catch his scent. The snake was far enough away that the buzz was merely a warning—*stay away.* Ben had every intention of doing so. Snorty hesitated and attempted to back away when the rattler announced himself, but Ben calmed the horse a bit, and, still somewhat nervous, Snorty sucked water in long, slurping draughts.

Ben wet his bandana and wiped his face with it, rubbing at the sweat and dirt. Then he wet both hands and ran them through his hair. He didn't want to show up at Lee's place with wet hair, but he knew the breeze and the sun would dry his shoulder-length locks before he reached the ranch.

He stood for a moment as Snorty drank, then he re-wet the bandana and wiped away the layer of dust that covered the leather vest he was wearing. His marshall's star was pinned to the left breast of the vest, and he ran the bandana over the badge too, removing the dirt. Even clean, it was dull—its subdued, flat-brass finish wouldn't reflect light as a silver badge would. Ben had seen a lieutenant at Antietam go down with a sniper's bullet through his heart because he had foolishly left his reflective insignia on his field jacket. Ben wouldn't make the same mistake.

He noticed a wispy brown mist—not quite a cloud—to the south and east as he swung into his saddle. *Another herd coming in to Burnt Rock.* The thought struck him like an unexpected punch. *Probably the Long Snake—the steer that killed Lee's horses must've slipped the herd.* He watched the sky for a long moment and then rode on toward the Busted Thumb. When he topped a rise a couple of miles from Lee's ranch, he reined in again.

The place looked, from his vantage point, like a toy farm arranged by a very meticulous child. The main barn stood straight and true, the fresh coat of red paint applied to it after the winter already weathering to a calm, almost pastel shade. The second barn—used for breeding and housing mares, foals, and injured or ill horses—had been painted too. What looked like miles of double-rail fence cut the land into neat squares and rectangles, each with anywhere from eight or ten to twenty or more horses grazing inside. Lee's house, a white, two-story structure with a front porch, faced away from the barns, and some sort of colorful wildflowers grew neatly around the foundation.

Carlos and Maria's house was fifty yards away from Lee's, and a bit closer to the barns. Carlos had been with the Busted Thumb since its first days. He was more than

35

an asset to the ranch—he was a trusted friend. And Maria was the finest cook Ben had ever known.

Beyond the fences and buildings were about four hundred acres of decent grazing that was for the most part unfenced. The grass still looked spring-lush, but in a month or so the summer sun would bake much of the color from it, and the horses would need to eat more to maintain weight and health.

Ben let Snorty pick his way down the slope and then put him into a lope toward the buildings. Carlos, riding an eye-catching red roan horse that was giving him an argument about something, waved to Ben from the pasture behind the main barn. Ben returned the wave and jigged Snorty into a gallop, closing the distance between him and his friend on the fractious horse. Now Ben saw that the red roan was rearing, trying to unseat his rider. Carlos, sitting as comfortably as he would in an overstuffed armchair, rode out the animal's tantrum.

The red stallion sunfished a few more times, but his bucks and jumps lacked the power they'd exhibited earlier. The argument was over. Carlos put the young stallion through a few rapid figure eights and then reined him over to Ben.

The men shook hands. "Good to see you, Ben." Carlos looked into the horizon. "Hey, look at thees!" He pointed to the smudge in the sky to the southeast.

"Yeah. I noticed. It's another herd comin' in, and a big one at that. I figure it's the Long Snake."

"I rode by the yards two days ago. No more cattle can go in there."

"The scouts for that drive must've gotten word back to their ramrod about the yards. They'll set up a camp out on the prairie. I'll pay them a visit in the morning."

"What you gonna tell them, Ben? They gonna wanna ship, an' there ees no bridge."

"The only thing I can tell them is to move on. I can't let them stay anywhere near town with a herd. They ain't gonna like it, but they'll have to drive on to Benton Center." He paused. "I heard about the mares and the Long Snake steer."

Carlos nodded. "Ees bad business, Ben. *Muy mal.* Lee, she only talk about the mares an' foals, but she could've been killed. A *loco* steer don' see no difference between a horse an' a lady when he ees lookin' for blood."

Ben nodded. "Yeah. I know. A cowboy tussled with a bull on Main Street today. Doc says it'll cost him the use of his leg, an' his horse was killed. If that had been Lee . . ." He swallowed hard and tried to let the thought drop.

"But ees three hundred miles to Benton Center, an' not much good pasture. The beef, they weel lose weight."

"That can't be helped." Ben forced a smile. "We can't do nothin' about it now. Let's let it go till tomorrow."

"I weel ride out with you, no?"

"If you can spare the time, I'd appreciate it. You still have your badge from last time?"

"*Sí*—I have it." He paused for a moment, staring at the sky, and then looked at Ben. "You're right—let's enjoy tonight, an' tomorrow weel be tomorrow, no?" Carlos's smile looked a bit forced. "Lee tol' us you were coming. Maria has been cooking an' baking all the day." He swung his horse away from Ben. "Les' put these boys in stalls with good hay an' fresh water an' we weel visit."

"Sounds good. I'll say hello to Lee and be back in a few minutes."

Carlos grinned. "Lee ees more *importante* than Maria's coffee?"

"Well . . . don't tell Maria that, okay?"

Lee's smile when she opened the door was almost enough to chase all the bad things out of Ben's world. She stepped back inside, closed the door, and welcomed his hug. After a moment they parted and stood looking into one another's eyes. Spoken words couldn't have been as eloquent.

As always, Lee's beauty made Ben struggle for breath. She wasn't perfect, like the women pictured on the posters for stage plays and recitals. Nor was she delicate and doe-eyed. She was tall for a lady of the time—5'7"—and she was leaner than the plump form currently in fashion. Her features were even but not classical, and her dark hair swept the mid-point of her back. But her eyes were magic—the darkest liquid chestnut, penetrating at times, as soft as a butterfly's whisper at other times.

The relationship between him and Lee had begun almost six years ago, when Lee purchased the land and buildings that were now the Busted Thumb Horse Farm. There had been some rough roads in their romance. And Ben knew the fact that they had not yet taken the natural and godly step to marriage indicated that some problems still existed. But then, both were as fiercely independent as hawks and cherished that independence.

"I'm glad you could make it," Lee said.

"Me too. I haven't seen you since Sunday. That's too long."

Lee laughed. "That's only three days, Ben."

"Like I said—too long."

She took his hand and led him into the parlor. "Coffee?" she asked.

"No, no thanks. Carlos promised me a cup. I'm going over to his place after the two of us talk for a bit."

Lee settled herself in a rocking chair, facing Ben on the sofa. "Willy found you? You heard about what happened here?"

"Yeah. I don't like the way that was handled, Lee. You should have sent for me right away."

"To do what?"

"I could've—"

"There was nothing you could do. It was all over." She smiled at him. "You can't be my private lawman, Ben Flood. You have a town to watch over."

He was silent for a long moment. "Yes, I can. And I am."

Lee crossed the room and sat next to him on the sofa. "Yes, I know that," she whispered. "And I love you for it." She let her hand rest on his shoulder for a moment before speaking again. "I heard the stockyard is full."

"Overfull. There's another big herd on its way in too. It's probably the one that the steer that killed your horses came from. I'm gonna send them on to Benton Center tomorrow. I asked Carlos to ride along with me."

"Good. What about all the cattle in the yards?"

Ben sighed. "I'm gonna have to send them on too. No way round it."

"None of them will like it, Ben. But there's no option, is there? They can't wait around for the bridge to be rebuilt." She paused. "Can they?"

"I dunno what they'll do. There's a lot of rough country and sparse pasture between here and Benton Center. That'll cost a lot in terms of lost weight, and they're bound to lose some stock on the way. I'm afraid they'll decide to keep their herds outside town and let 'em graze on the good grass until the bridge is up."

Lee appeared to be thinking over what he'd said. "That wouldn't be good, would it?"

39

"Not at all. Those longhorns are pure crazy, and havin' them within a few miles of town scares me. The cowhands are a problem themselves too, a problem Burnt Rock doesn't need."

"Then you've got to turn them away, right?"

"Yeah. But I'm afraid of starting a sort of range war between Burnt Rock and the cattlemen. That'd cause a lot of bloodshed."

Lee sighed, stood, and faced Ben. "Well, there's nothing you can do about it right now. Why not go over to Carlos's and brag to each other about your horses? I've got to finish up the soup I'm bringing over at dinnertime, and clean myself up too."

Ben stood and reached out to embrace her. He could have stood there forever inhaling the fresh, sunny scent of her hair and reveling in her closeness to him.

When they stepped back, neither spoke for a quiet moment.

Lee broke the silence. "Go get your coffee. I have work to do."

Ben groaned and pushed back from Maria's table, which was still heavily burdened with dishes, plates, and bowls containing the highly spiced Mexican meals for which she was famous.

"You don' like my *tamales?*" Maria asked.

"No, Maria, I don't," Ben said, burping discreetly behind his hand. "I ate five of them just to make sure your feelings wouldn't be hurt."

"Ees not spicy enough thees night, Maria," Carlos complained. "The *aroz con pollo* had no flavor to it— like gringo food."

Ben groaned again. "The chicken and rice was perfect, Maria. Don't listen to Carlos. He knows nothing about Mexican food."

Lee laughed out loud. "You two men attacked this meal the way hogs go at a trough. And Carlos, if the *pollo* wasn't hot enough, why did you drink four glasses of water with it?"

"Ees no true."

Ben pushed up from his chair and walked to Maria's side. He leaned over and gave her a loud, smacking kiss on the cheek. "You get rid of that fat ol' man and we'll talk, okay, Maria?"

Lee stood too. "I'll walk you out to the barn, Ben. Maria, Carlos, thanks for a perfect meal and a fine evening."

"Yeah, thanks again," Ben added. "Everything was great." He put his hand on Carlos's shoulder. "See you early tomorrow."

"*Sí*. You bes' have coffee ready."

"You can count on that, Carlos," Ben said, opening the door for Lee. "Goodnight, Maria."

Lee and Ben walked slowly toward the barn. There were a couple of lanterns lit in the building, and two men were stacking hay in the rear.

Ben draped his blanket over Snorty's back, smoothing it carefully with his palms. When he hefted his saddle and eased it onto the blanket, Lee spoke.

"I'm worried about you, Ben. If those men decide to stay on, it'll mean nothing but trouble. I noticed how you and Carlos wouldn't talk about the herds at dinner. He's as worried as I am."

"I know. It scares me to have them anywhere near town or your ranch. One stampede would set them all off, and that'd be a disaster."

He reached out to shake her hand, and she smiled, knowing the reason for the handshake instead of a hug and a kiss. The two men working in the barn would carry tales all over West Texas if the boss lady was seen smoochin' the marshall.

Ben led Snorty outside and stepped into a stirrup. "Don't you worry," he said. "I can handle this."

She nodded. "I know, Ben. Just . . ."

"I'll be careful. I'm always careful. You know that." He started Snorty moving, tipped his hat to her, and rode off into the dark prairie.

Sure, you're careful, Ben—about as careful as a mama mountain cat protecting her babies. If anything ever happened to you . . .

She watched him and his horse until they disappeared into the night. Then she walked into her parlor and lit a small lamp, its cheerful light through the amber-colored shade raising her spirits a bit. She sat in her rocker and looked out the window at the darkness.

Conversation she couldn't quite make out and a low chuckle reached her from the bunkhouse. She pictured the men settling in for the night, ready for sleep and the next day that would follow. *I'm genuinely grateful for being so blessed with all of this. If only Ben could share more of it with me. If only he hadn't traded a normal life for that of a lawman . . .*

She put the thought aside. "Quit your whining," she said aloud. As she reached toward the Bible resting on the table next to her chair, a soft knocking sounded from the kitchen.

"Lee?" Maria called.

"Maria, come in. Is there a problem?"

42

Maria walked through the kitchen and sat on the sofa. "I saw Ben ride off, an' I saw you standin' there watchin' him too long."

Lee smiled at her perceptive friend. "I know. I guess I'm still spooked by what happened to the mares. And I could see in Ben's eyes that he's expecting bad trouble with the cattlemen."

"Carlos, he too ees 'fraid. Still, they weel go to that camp an' do what they need to do, an' leave us to the worryin' 'bout them. Men, I think, are sometimes dumb, no? Even your Ben—he know you love heem, an' he could marry you an' be aroun' the horses he also love, an' no carry his *pistola* all the time. He could have all that, an' yet he risks his life every day for his town. It don' make no sense."

"He's a good man, Maria. A good Christian man."

"I know thees. But he ees the same as any man—stubborn as a goat. Carlos too. All men."

Their eyes met across the small room. The image of Carlos as a goat made Lee giggle, and Maria joined in. When their chortling slowed and then ended, there was a precious warmth in the room that forbade tears or trepidation.

"Shall we pray together, Maria?" Lee asked, again reaching for her Bible.

"Thees ees why I come to you tonight—to laugh an' to pray, goats or no goats."

3

Carlos, riding the big, affable red roan he'd named Happy, saw the light in Snorty's shelter behind the marshall's office and slowed his mount to a walk. The heady scent of his friend's coffeepot drew Carlos as a magnet does steel shavings, but he swung Happy in a wide arc and rode slowly back in the direction from which he'd come. Carlos knew Ben's procedure for starting a day, and even with his craving for a couple of mugs of Arbuckle's Dark Roast, he wouldn't approach the shelter quite yet.

Ben sat on a bale of hay with his back against the unfinished boards that made up one side of the lean-to. A hissing, sputtering kerosene lantern hung from a nail a couple of feet over his head, casting its harsh white light over the Bible that was open on his lap. Ben's head was back, his Stetson on the floor next to him. His eyes were closed, but he was far from asleep. In fact, almost all his physical senses were engaged by his surroundings. He reveled in the scent of well-cared-for leather, the sweet smell of the stacked hay, the morning sounds of Snorty shuffling his hooves and huffing through his nostrils. Even the texture of the smooth and creamy pages of the Bible sang out to him that the world was good because God had made it that way.

Snorty picked Happy's scent out of the still air and blew loudly through his nostrils in greeting. Ben opened his eyes, carefully closed his Bible, and stood, placing the book on a clean shelf next to a can of hoof balm. He was ready for the day.

He headed over to his office. While he was filling a pair of chipped ceramic mugs with coffee that looked more than a little hot as it glistened in the lantern light, Carlos walked into the room. The two men sipped for a few moments before speaking.

"Ees no much on flavor, but ees hot an' strong," Carlos commented.

Ben grinned. "It'll wake you up and get you ready to ride, that's for sure." He noticed the brass deputy's badge pinned to Carlos's vest. "I guess we're all official."

"Sí. What do you know 'bout thees herd we go to?"

"Not much. One of the boys at O'Keefe's says the Long Snake has better'n a thousand head. The ramrod's called Atticus Toole. The fella said there's supposed to be some paper on him back in Arkansas for burning a farmhouse. If there is, I haven't heard about it. I sent a wire."

"Could be a bad man, then."

"Maybe. Or the hand I was talkin' to may have just been runnin' his mouth and spreadin' a rumor."

"Can't tell with *vaqueros,* Ben. Could be thees man got fired an' jus' don' like Toole."

"Could be. But it's a sure bet we're not gonna find out anything standin' round here jawin'. Ready to ride?"

Carlos slugged down the rest of his coffee as if it were a dose of vile-tasting medicine. "Ready as I weel ever be," he said.

The morning air was fresh and invigorating, and the horses wanted to stretch their muscles. The men put their mounts into a lope and then a gallop, Carlos holding Happy back ten yards behind Ben. Snorty, the faster of the two horses by far, would drive Ben crazy if he and Carlos attempted to gallop side by side.

The sun was peeking up from beyond the horizon, frightening away the delicate pastels that had preceded it. Dew on the prairie glinted and sparkled like countless tiny stars in the new light. And in Ben's mind, the cool scent of the open land smelled better than the finest meal.

Soon Ben could hear the sound made by a thousand head of cattle confined to a few acres of grazing. It was really more of a physical sensation than something he could hear. The atmosphere *thrummed* with the presence of so many huge, hostile living creatures, and the very earth moved with the herd's shifting currents. *"Them longhorns knows they's goin' to the sledgehammer an' the knife, an' they're right sad about it,"* an old cowboy had once told him. He shook the image away—it wasn't at all a pleasant one.

The bleached canvas top of the chuck wagon was as visible as a white sail against a blue sea on the far side of a group of about two hundred cattle being handled by four mounted cowboys. The riders' horses were constantly in motion, turning to block wandering cattle, skittering away from the attacks of angry steers, keeping the herd bunched as tightly together as the longhorns would stand for without fighting among themselves. The cowhands' shirts were dark with sweat, and the chests and flanks of their horses frothy and dripping.

Ben and Carlos swung around the end of the cluster of cattle and rode at a walk to the chuck wagon. Ben watched the cowhands work. "Those boys are handy, and they're mounted real well too. Those horses know the job as well as the men do."

"Ees true," Carlos agreed. "An' ees better to watch than to do, no? Not much work that ees harder."

A lean, shirtless man stepped away from the wagon, a mug of coffee in one hand and an almost-raw beefsteak in the other. He tore into the meat with teeth that were very white and quite even—a rarity among cowboys. His hair—shiny ebony that showed no gray at all—reached almost to his belt and was worn in two braids. His body was well muscled, sinewy and hard, and he moved with the liquid grace of a cougar. Ben's eyes flicked to the Smith and Wesson .45 in a supple-looking holster tied to the man's right leg. The butt of the pistol rested just about where his fingers and palm could fall to it quickly.

Ben and Carlos reined in and let the man approach them. "Atticus Toole?" Ben asked.

"That's me, Marshall." The man nodded to the two riders. "How 'bout you boys slide down an' drink some coffee? You had chow yet today?" His voice was easy and pleasant, welcoming in tone and texture. His dark eyes were set in a strong, high-cheekboned face and neither confirmed nor denied the friendliness of his words.

"Coffee sounds good," Ben said, swinging down from his saddle. "My name's Ben Flood. I'm the lawman outta

48

Burnt Rock." He turned his head to Carlos. "This here's Carlos Montoya, my deputy."

Toole tore off another bite of steak. The blood from the meat dripped down his arm. He chewed for a half minute and swallowed a lump the size of a boy's fist. "Some problem out here, Marshall, or was you just ridin' by?"

Ben gathered Snorty's reins and led him toward the chuck wagon. "Let's get that java," he said. "An' Mr. Toole—you know the problem just as well as I do."

They walked the few yards to the wagon, and Ben and Carlos tied their horses to the rail. Toole gnawed another chunk from his steak and tossed the remainder—fat, bone, and gristle—into the cook's pot, which was already heating some stew for the noon meal.

Toole poured the coffee. "I ain't at all sure what you mean, Marshall."

"One thing is that I hear you might be a wanted man," Ben said.

Toole grinned, again showing the brightness of his teeth. "That's pure skunkwater, Marshall. I got me a pardon from the governor of Arkansas, all signed and sealed properlike. Wanna see it, or do you trust my word?"

"You know I need to see it."

Toole shrugged. "It don't make me no nevermind either way. I've showed it so many times, it's near wore out." He paused for a moment. "Now, what I gotta do is reach to my back pocket. You seem a tad nervous to me, Flood, so I thought I'd tell you that. I didn't want you to think I was about to pull my iron. I got a waterproof purse, like I said, in my pocket. Okay with you?"

Ben took a step back from Toole. His posture didn't change, but his right hand dropped almost casually to his side. "Fine with me."

Carlos not quite as casually moved a few feet to the side. Toole tugged a waxed-leather document case from his pocket, unfolded the three sections of it, and removed a paper with the seal of the State of Arkansas at the top. He handed it to Ben, who read the page carefully and then handed it back to Toole.

"Good," he said. "Sorry."

"No need to be sorry," Toole said. "I burned that house down sure's you're standin' there, Flood. I done some work for the governor, an' he took care of the charge. Now, what's the other problem you got?"

"You can't stay here with your herd. You gotta move on to Benton Center or somewhere else, and you gotta do it soon."

He could see a subtle change in Atticus Toole. It was as if the planes of his face had somehow become sharper, more prominent, and his eyes took on a bit of luster that hadn't been there a moment ago. "Nope," he said.

"I wasn't askin' you, Toole. I was tellin' you. You gotta move this herd."

"You an' your deputy gonna chase me away? I got almost a hundred men here. We ain't goin' nowhere. The owner of the Long Snake Cattle Company sent a messenger here to tell me to set tight with his cattle until further notice, an' that's what I'm gonna do."

"We'll see," Ben said. He placed his half-full mug on the tailgate of the wagon. Carlos did the same. "One more thing," Ben said. "A steer with the Long Snake brand on it killed two real good mares on a horse ranch not too far from here. Both mares were heavy in foal. Neither of the horses killed were for sale—they were foundation breeding stock. And the owner of those horses was in great danger. She's a friend of mine, Toole. A real good friend. That makes this personal."

50

Toole laughed. "Musta been some rustler run off one of my beefs." He chuckled again. "Say, if it ain't too much trouble, could you run my steer back out here for me? That's part of your job, ain't it? Returnin' stuff to its rightful owners?"

"Don't push your luck, Toole."

"Luck? I don't need no luck dealin' with lawmen or Mexicans. How good do you think you are, Flood?"

"Good enough to drop you and that man over there cradlin' the shotgun before you clear leather."

"My, my." Toole laughed again. "Ain't you somethin'?"

Ben and Carlos mounted. "You've had your warning," Ben said. "I want this herd out of here."

Carlos reined Happy away from the chuck wagon, and Ben followed on Snorty.

"Ees a hard man," Carlos said when they were out of hearing range of the camp.

"Maybe. But we're harder."

"Ees no as many of us, though."

"Well, that's a point," Ben admitted.

Ben and Carlos rode up to the main barn at the Busted Thumb well after dark. The heat of the day hung damply in the air; the horses were sweated and tired and so were the men. Both realized that Toole was more than bluster and bravado—he'd have to be to head up a drive that size. Carlos and Ben had faced killers eye to eye before, and Atticus Toole, they realized, would have no more difficulty putting a bullet into their hearts than he would stepping on an ant.

Swinging by the other camps was time-consuming and frustrating. Nothing had changed. Ben and Carlos were both tired of the sight, sound, and smell of cattle—and the thick clouds of dust the herds raised.

Lee met them as they dismounted at the Busted Thumb. Even in the sputtering light of the lantern hung outside the barn, her eyes betrayed her concern. "I've got coffee and stew inside," she said. "You probably haven't eaten anything since morning. Come on, we'll talk in the kitchen."

Lee's kitchen, as always, was inviting. The little breeze that meandered by every so often barely moved the gingham curtains at the open windows, but the room was cooler and less humid than the air outside. The lamps—one in the doorway to the living room and the other over the table—cast a yellow light that was less harsh than the lanterns used in the barns.

The men attacked the stew as if they hadn't eaten in days, scooping large chunks of beef, carrots, and potato from their plates with inch-thick slabs of bread still warm from the oven. Maria hovered over the two men, refilling water glasses, ladling stew, cutting bread, but saying little. Lee sipped at a cup of coffee.

"Great stew," Ben said, pushing the plate away. It was as clean as it would have been had a hound licked up every scrap of meat and gravy.

"It should be. It cost me two mares and two unborn foals." Lee's words were harsh, but her voice was soft.

For a long moment, the kitchen was so silent that Ben could hear the almost inaudible squeaking of the bats devouring insects outside the house.

He stood, went around the table, and stood next to Carlos, his hand on his friend's shoulder. "I came to a decision today," he said. "Your work is with Lee and the horses here. I appreciate your being with me today, but Maria and Lee and the Busted Thumb have to come first. And this thing is bigger than I thought. I knew there'd be trouble, but I didn't know how much. Lee's horses slaughtered, that cowboy almost killed on Main Street, Toole's bloodthirstiness, the possibility of stampede—this whole thing could blow up right in my face. Your job is here, Carlos, just like mine is to protect my town."

"Sit, Ben," Lee urged. "Let's the three of us take a close look at what's happening."

Maria, now sitting next to her husband, covered his hand with her own but didn't speak. Her eyes and her face reflected the deep relief she felt at Ben's words.

"Or what could happen, no?" Carlos said. "I am but one *hombre*, an' I belong in two places all at once."

"I'll call you if I need to, Carlos. I promise you that. But for now, you have a horse farm to manage."

Carlos finished his mug of coffee. Lee moved to the stove and refilled his mug, Ben's, and her own. She gently pushed Ben toward the chair he'd vacated.

"Luke ees a good man, a smart man," Carlos said. "If I need to go with Ben, he weel keep the Thumb safe— keep Maria an' Lee an' our horses safe. Thees I know."

Ben settled into his chair. "Luke ain't you, Carlos, but he's a good man," he agreed.

"Can there be no peace with the herders, Ben?" Maria asked. "If they stay out on the prairie an' watch their cows, why there mus' be trouble?"

Lee nodded her head. "Maria has a good point. What happened in town and here could have been prevented— no doubt about that. Each of the herds has a full crew, haven't they? If they could control their beef on the trail, can't they contain them here? Even if they summer here and wait for the temporary bridge, there's enough pasture out there to support the stock."

"That sounds good, but ees no true," Carlos interjected.

"How so?"

Ben leaned over in his chair. "One big difference is the fact that Burnt Rock is too close to those herds for safety. You know the sorts of thunderstorms we get all summer, Lee. If one herd stampeded, all of them would."

"But the herds are miles apart. How could—"

"Ben, he ees right, Lee," Carlos said. "I see thees myself with the buffalo herds when I wass a boy. The earth shake an' tremble when so many animals move, an' the ground, she carry the fear, the . . . how do you say . . . the . . . ?"

"Panic," Ben said. "Yeah. I've seen it too. It's uncanny—one big herd starts runnin', and within minutes it's like some demon was layin' leather to the backs of the other herds anywhere within miles around." He sighed. "And I don't know if a possible stampede is even the biggest problem. There are maybe two hundred of the wildest men the frontier has ever seen out there with the herds. Lots of them are deserters from both sides of the War, and lots of them are runnin' from the law. Too many of them are too plumb crazy to do anything but move longhorns. They've got money to spend—I heard tell most of 'em have been paid for the drive an' been given a bonus for stayin' on with the herds on top of it. There's nowhere to use that money but Burnt Rock—an' it's a sure bet they'll all head to the Drovers' Inn like kids with a penny head to the candy counter. When those men get liquored up, it's like the gates of hell opened up to get rid of its worst prisoners."

Lee's eyes widened as Ben spoke. Carlos's face was hard as he nodded his head the slightest bit at his friend's words.

"What can you do, Ben?" Lee asked.

"I'm not sure yet. When I get back to town tonight, I'll drag the Western Union man outta bed and get a wire

54

off to Fort Kaiser. If the general there can send me even a couple dozen well-armed men, it could make all the difference in the world."

"What about shutting down the saloon?" Lee asked.

"That was my first idea, 'til I thought it through. A sign sayin' 'closed' ain't gonna bother those men. If I tried to stop them . . . well . . ."

Lee shuddered in spite of the warmth in the room. "There's one thing we can do," she said quietly.

Ben focused his eyes on her face. She folded her hands on the table in front of her.

"Pray," she said.

Lee watched Ben ride off and then returned to her kitchen. It was difficult for her to sit still; her mind refused to cast away the images of her dead horses and the weariness—and trepidation—in Ben's eyes. She took the lamp hanging over the window and carried it to her office. The safe under the long library table hulked in the shadows like a gargoyle until she set the lamp on the floor and the safe's squared lines defined it as a benign steel box. She worked the combination from memory and grunted at the weight of the door as she eased it open. The safe was short enough to fit under the table, but it weighed eight hundred pounds. Carlos had needed to add a pillar under the floor in the cellar to support it, and it had taken four good men to move the safe from the freight wagon to Lee's office.

She moved the lamp closer. The deed to her land, the ownership papers for Slick, and receipts for at least fifty other horses rested in a neat stack. A cash box containing operating capital faced Lee. Behind it was a cloth sack of gold eagles that was satisfyingly heavy as she moved it aside. What she was after was at the very rear of the safe.

The wooden box—finely crafted and lacquered—was about the size of a novel. The words "Colt Firearm Company, Hartford, Connecticut" were lettered in fine gold script and reflected the lantern light softly. She remembered her uncle Noah's words as he'd handed the box to her. *"Texas can be rough, honey. A lady needs protection. You're good with a long gun and a side arm, but there could be a time when you'll need a little extra help. This will kick like a burned mule—hold it in both hands or it'll break your wrist—and it doesn't have any accuracy beyond six or eight feet. But it could save your life."*

Lee opened the box. The derringer itself was an ugly little thing, barely four inches long. The two barrels, one atop the other, gaped like a pair of empty sockets in a skull. There was no trigger guard, but both triggers required a strong yank, far stronger than what could happen by accident. The small grips were mother of pearl, but that aesthetic touch didn't make the weapon any less deadly. The pistol rested upon a supple calfskin holster to which long, half-inch-wide straps of latigo were attached with tight saddlemaker's stitches. The custom-designed rig was meant to be worn under a blouse or shirt, at the small of a woman's back. Getting to the gun wouldn't be quick, but it was an emergency weapon—a "hide out" to be drawn only as a last resort.

Lee tugged the tail of her work shirt out of the waist of her culottes and fit the holster and weapon at her back. She drew the latigo tight and retucked her shirt. The derringer felt like a turtle attempting to climb her back, but she knew she'd get used to it.

The image of her dead mares resurfaced in her mind. Unconsciously, her right hand reached behind, and her fingers touched the outline of the holster.

Snorty moved well as he headed out from the Busted Thumb. Although Ben had covered many miles on the big stallion in the course of the day, Snorty seemed as fresh as he had before the sun had risen that morning.

The moon was at three-quarter phase, and the prairie spread before man and horse like a placid pool of dark water, featureless and calm. Ben rode easily to his mount's lope, his mind scrambling to make sense out of what faced him, to form a plan of some sort that would give him a fighting chance against the herds.

Snorty picked up the scent of a horse before Ben could make out the shadowy form of a man standing next to his mount at the edge of a small pool. Ben reined in and slid his right boot out of his stirrup, letting his leg hang free. He had no idea who the man was or if he offered any danger, but with the way things were going, he wanted the quickest access to his .45 possible. He touched the grips of his weapon.

"Ho, the rider!" A strangely familiar voice called from the water hole. "Ride on in an' drink. Ain't no trouble gonna come to you."

Ben jigged his mount ahead at a walk. The stranger's horse whinnied a greeting to Snorty, and Snorty huffed in response. The fellow began to crouch over, and Ben's .45 was in his hand, the muzzle centered on the stranger's chest.

"Whooooeee!" the rider exclaimed, raising both his hands over his head. "Don't you go gunnin' me, friend—I ain't even armed. I was jist hunkerin' down to get me a drink is all."

Ben stepped down, his Colt still in his hand but lowered now, next to his holster. He took a few steps forward, and Snorty paced behind him. "Can't be too careful out here," he said. "Just let me get in a little closer an' I'll—"

"Hey! Ain't you Marshall Flood? It's me—Hubbard Mott. We seen each other at the stockyard, 'member?"

"Sure, I remember, Hubbard," Ben answered, holstering his weapon. "What're you doing way out here this time of night?" Before Mott spoke up, Ben added, "Sorry about pullin' iron on you, partner, but like I said, a man can't be too careful."

"'Specially a lawman, I guess. No harm done, Marshall."

Ben walked closer to the wrangler and extended his hand. Mott took it, and they shook hands.

"So, I'll ask again: What're you doin' out in the middle of nowhere?"

"Well, I'll tell ya, Marshall, the boys got quite a poker game goin' by the yards. I figured the mix of cards an' whiskey an' that bunch means there's gonna be lead in the air 'fore the night's over. An' I got the day off tomorrow, so I rode on out an' brung my blanket. I'll sleep out here somewheres an' won't have no drunken cowhands to worry about."

Ben laughed. "Makes good sense, Hubbard."

"Sure, it does. Nice an' peaceful out here. Seems to me folks need more peace in their lives, Marshall."

"World's gettin' smaller every day, Hubbard. Seems like there's not much peace around anymore."

"There's places, Marshall. A fella jist gotta know where to look."

Ben nodded. "Look, I'm wonderin' if you'd care to earn ten dollars, Hubbard."

The wrangler smiled, his three front teeth clear in the moonlight. "I might, Marshall, dependin' on what you got in mind."

Ben led Snorty to the edge of the pool and waited as he lowered his head and began to suck water. "I need to get the ramrods of the drives—yours, the Nines, Long Snake, all the others—to meet with me tomorrow at noon in my office in Burnt Rock. I've already put a bunch of miles on my horse today, an' I need some sleep myself if I'm gonna meet with that crew. If you'd care to carry my message to each of them, I'd pay you that ten dollars an' thank you for your trouble."

"What exactly you want me to tell them, Marshall?"

"Just this: Be there at noon, or you'll regret you weren't. And . . . no, that's all. Be there at noon, or you'll regret you weren't."

"That's a lotta ridin'. The Long Snake's way out, an' so's the Double D."

"Ten dollars is a lotta money too."

"Well," Mott considered, "it is, ain't it? I'll tell you what, Marshall—make it fifteen, an' I'll head out right now."

Ben grinned. "Twelve."

"Done! Uhhh—one thing. Ain't nobody gonna be shootin' at me, is there? I know everybody's got night riders out, but I don't want to catch a slug jist for car-ryin' a message."

"Just announce yourself an' you'll be fine. No reason for anyone to gun you."

Mott smiled again. "I'll say me a little prayer 'fore I ride into each of them camps, anyways."

Ben was surprised. "You a prayin' man, Hubbard?"

The cowboy seemed to stand a little taller and a little straighter in the feeble light of the moon. "I was brung to Jesus Christ eleven years ago, an' I been with him ever since."

"That's really—"

59

"Some of the other Christians I come across, they kinda look down on me 'cause I follow cattle butts for my pay an' can't read or do sums good. I'll tell you the same thing I tell them: The Lord don't care what one of his children does for a livin', long as he does it honest an' with a good heart." He glared at Ben and raised an admonishing finger. "An' Jesus didn't have no trouble ridin' with fishermen an' sodbusters an' so forth, now did he? Why—"

"Hold on, Hubbard!" Ben laughed. "I'm a Christian too, and I know exactly what you mean. Some of the finest Christians I know are wranglers and so forth. Lookit me—I'm a lawman in a dusty little town that nobody's ever heard of. We all come to the Lord from different places, partner."

A moment went by before Mott broke into a laugh. "Guess I'm kinda preachin' to the choir. But look, since we're both Christians, let's say a few words to the Lord before we go on our different ways, okay?"

The rest of the trip back to Burnt Rock took on the mindless monotony that a long ride at night always did. Ben settled into the easy, softly rocking motion of Snorty's lope, letting the drumming of hooves on the prairie floor lull him into a half-sleep, completely confident that his horse knew where they were going and would get them there.

When they were almost home, Ben stood in his stirrups and leaned forward to swipe a hand across his horse's chest. Snorty's coat was still damp, but it was rapidly crusting with dried sweat. A hard rubdown with a coarse grain sack, a flake of timothy hay, and a half bucket of fresh water would make the horse feel like new. As for himself, the cot in the first cell of his jail was at least as inviting as a bed in Buckingham Palace.

If Ben had been a man to curse, the series of pistol shots that echoed over the prairie from town would have elicited a whole string of cusswords. Snorty was digging in and running hard almost before Ben finished applying the leg pressure that gave the command. There were more shots, followed by the strangely musical tinkle of breaking glass.

Ben drew the Winchester 30.30 from the scabbard attached to his saddle at his right knee and entered Main Street at the end farthest from the Drovers' Inn. He levered a round into the rifle's chamber as Snorty covered the length of the darkened town. The only light showing was that of the saloon, a yellowish illumination that wept through the clouds of tobacco smoke and out the batwing doors.

A cluster of eight or ten men stood in the street in front of the gin mill, all of them facing the alley that ran between Scott's Mercantile and the next building, which housed Thelma's Lady's Finery and Bailey's Butcher and Provisions Shop. Three men had pistols in their hands, and several others held bottles.

Ben's lawman instincts told him the problem here was drunkenness, not violence. The postures of all the men were sloppy, their laughter and hoots and rebel yells exaggerated not by anger but by alcohol. The moonlight caught the jagged edges of the three windows that fronted Thelma's, and shards and bits of glass glittered on the wooden sidewalk. One of the men raised his pistol, pointing the barrel straight up. Ben squeezed his trigger before the drunk could fire. The authoritative boom of the rifle turned all eyes to him. "Put up those guns!" he roared.

Ben touched Snorty's bit with the lightest tug on the reins, setting the horse up for a fast stop. A high-pitched squeal sliced through the silence following his round and his yell. He looked to the alley perhaps ten feet in front of him as he barreled toward the mob. Another squeal—this one longer, louder—issued from the alley, and then, much too quickly for Ben to react, a fat boar hog scrambled into Main Street directly in front of Snorty. The hog skidded to a stop, its massive, mud-encrusted body like a low wall in front of Ben. It was too late for Ben to respond, too late for him to swing Snorty to either side—too late to do anything.

But it wasn't too late for Snorty. He launched himself into the air like a mountain cat taking down a deer, pushing himself off the ground with all the power of his rear legs and hurling his body upward and forward. The boar screeched again as Snorty's left front shoe touched its ear, slicing an almost surgical notch into the delicate tissue. The quick pain was enough to unfreeze the hog from its panicked paralysis. It dashed across the street and soon was lost in the darkness of the prairie.

A wide, powerfully thrown loop whistled past Snorty's rump while he was still in the air. In a heartbeat a rider, his horse in full flight, blasted out of the mouth of the alley.

Snorty landed hard, slightly off balance, and Ben instinctively leaned with the horse, using his body weight to help Snorty regain his stability. Then Ben jumped off and waded into the group of men, swinging his fists and using his shoulders like a battering ram.

The roper who'd been after the boar jammed his horse around in a leaning, scrambling turn and spurred back to the melee, aiming for Ben. Ben snatched a half-full bottle of whiskey from a downed cowboy and pitched it at the mounted man, catching him in the middle of his chest and slamming him from his saddle. The roper's horse, now riderless and quirted by terror, veered past the cursing, punching turmoil of men and galloped beyond the end of the street.

Ben threw an attacker into the path of two others, dropping all three of them. He used a roundhouse right hand to stop another cowboy but was hit from the side by yet another. Ben's elbow spread that cowboy's nose wide open with an audible snapping of cartilage. He took a step back. The next man lurched to a clumsy halt, his eyes on the gaping barrel of the Colt .45 that had so suddenly appeared in Ben's hand.

"Down on the ground!" Ben gasped, sucking air to fill his starved lungs. "Gimme a reason to gun you, an' I will! Down—all of you!"

He could now see how many brawlers there were. Four from Harmon Kenny's Double D drive and the other five from Atticus Toole's Long Snake herd. Ben marched them in single file to the back door of his office, had them shuck their gun belts and pistols, and then searched them individually, finding five boot knives, two pairs of brass knuckles, two blackjacks, and three partially consumed pints of whiskey. He jammed all nine of the surly, cursing men into a single cell.

"Hey," complained one, "we ain't gonna be able to sleep here. There ain't enough room to lay down."

"That's a real shame," Ben said. "Maybe you'll think before you tear up my town again."

"An' maybe I'll rip your head off an' stuff it down your neck when you open this cage tomorrow," a coarse voice challenged.

Ben looked over the gang of cowboys. "Why wait till tomorrow? Wanna try it right now?" When there was no response, he strode to the front of the office and out to the street to fetch Snorty.

He hated to do it, but he went over and pounded on the Western Union office door until the clerk, sleepy-eyed and befuddled, lumbered out from the small room he slept in at the rear of the single-story building. The man held his lamp at chest height and cracked open the door. When he saw Ben's badge in the lamplight, he opened the door all the way.

"Emergency, Ben?" he asked.

"I wouldn't have bothered you at this time of night if it wasn't. I need three wires to go out right away."

The clerk became all business. "Yessir. Let's do it, then."

A half hour later, Ben rubbed down his horse in the lean-to behind his office, fed him a flake of hay and a scoop of oats and molasses, and hung a bucket of water in his stall.

He then arranged a bed for himself by lining up some baled hay and tossing a ragged blanket over it. After removing his Stetson and his gun belt, he stretched out. There'd be noise and trouble as his nine captives tried to find some sleeping space in the small cell, and he didn't care to hear it or to attempt to sort it out.

He turned out his prisoners first thing in the morning to avoid the cost of feeding them. He charged each one a twenty-dollar fine for disturbing the peace and told them they could pick up their weapons in a week, if they were still in town. "If it was up to me," he added, "I'd dump your guns down a deep well and run the whole slew of you outta Burnt Rock. Give me any more trouble, an' that's exactly what I'll do."

There was some grumbling about the fines and the treatment they'd received from the lawman, but there was nothing even close to a challenge from any of them. The cowboys looked even more motley in the light of day, and the rotgut they'd been drinking had erupted from several of them during the night. Ben counted four blackened eyes, a pair of crushed noses, and several gaps in front teeth. He didn't bother to stifle his smile as the crew shuffled out the back door.

He lost the grin quickly as he began mopping the fetid, vomit-spotted cell. Even three good splashes from a gallon jug of bleach didn't seem to rid the jail of the vile odor. By the time he was finished, he had decided to head to the barbershop for a bath and a shave—never mind what the luxury would cost him.

But even as Ben was sinking into the tub of steaming water, bad news continued to dog him. "Three wires for the marshall . . ." Ben heard from the front of the barbershop. "I knowed he was here 'cause I seen him walk in just afore my receiver started up."

A moment later Ben read each of the three flimsy yellow half sheets. The answers to his requests for help from the cavalry and two other lawmen in other jurisdictions were what he'd expected: negative. He crumpled the wires, tossed them across the room, and allowed himself to sink under the surface of the water. At least until he had to come up for air, no one would be able to bother him.

A few hours later, Ben sat behind his desk, wearing a fresh shirt and clean denim pants. His face was still tingling from the razor, and he held a mug of O'Keefe's good coffee in front of him.

Atticus Toole strode in, slamming the door behind him much harder than necessary. "I'm here 'cause the Long Snake is a law-abidin' outfit, an' we cooperate with local law when we can. I'm also here 'cause the other ramrods voted me to represent their herds. The other ramrods are down to the Drovers' Inn waitin' on me. I'll tell them what we talk about. An' any decision I make binds them just like it does me an' my crew."

Ben nodded. "And I'm here because I represent the law of this state. Let's be clear on that."

Toole dragged the chair in front of Ben's desk out another foot or so and sat facing him. "Feisty today, ain't you, Flood?" he said with a smile. "Here I ride all this way to jaw with you when I got plenty of work to do, an' you can't keep a civil tongue in your head." His smile broadened. "Just don't seem right, Marshall Flood."

He shoved his chair back another foot and raised his boot heels onto the edge of Ben's desk. The dark, sticky substance on the soles of his boots showed that he hadn't been careful where he walked as he looked over his herd that morning.

"I heard you're a hard man, Flood," Toole said in a strangely conversational tone of voice. "I heard you was a terror durin' the war. An' I heard you gunned Zeb Stone in a fair fight in some Mex town. What I'm wonderin', Marshall, is should I be scared of you an' your big rep? See, I know for a fact you ain't gonna get no help from the army. The owner of the Snake has contacts. He says there ain't no way the army's gonna release a single man to play around with a town-an'-cattlemen dispute."

Ben stared for a long moment at Toole's boots. Then he returned the ramrod's smile. "I think maybe you should be afraid of me, Toole. Fact is, I think you should have nightmares about me that wake you up screamin' for your mama."

Toole laughed. At that same moment he found himself with his boots on the floor and the muzzle of Ben's

.45 pressing against his forehead. When Toole's hand darted toward the pistol holstered at his side, Ben, leaning over the desk, thumbed back the hammer of his Colt.

"Well," Toole said. "I gotta admit you move good."

"You done playin'? You ready to talk?"

Atticus Toole shoved his chair back, away from Ben's gun. His eyes had hardened to embers, and his voice was now rough, coarse, like a file scraping metal. "I'm done playin', but we got no talkin' to do. Me an' the others—the X2, the Double D, the Nine, Running M, the B-Dog—we ain't movin' our beef. The day we can ship our stock over the Dos Gatos is the day we're gone—but not till then. All the owners are behind us. That ground out there is open prairie. You got no right to—"

"Don't tell me about my rights," Ben snarled. "Go on back an' get your men and your cattle ready to move. Provision up with what you need and head out. Now, get outta my office an' outta my town." He eased down the hammer and put his Colt in his holster, maintaining eye contact with the cattleman.

Toole's smirk returned, but his eyes didn't change. "Like I said earlier, you're feisty today, Marshall." He turned, walked to the door, stopped, and turned back. "By the way," he added, "your throat looked awful good when you was bent over the desk, lawman." He flicked his right wrist with a sharp, short motion, and a stiletto appeared from under his sleeve. "I coulda stuck you like a pig."

"Before I could squeeze my trigger?"

"I think so."

"I'd bet a year's pay you couldn't. Now get out of my office."

"We ain't done, Flood. That's one thing you *can* bet on."

4

Lee rode Slick away from the main barn of the Busted Thumb and put him into a lope when she'd cleared the outbuildings of her ranch. The splendor of the West Texas early morning was lost on her today, as was the whisper of cooler air that had moved in overnight. Two cowhands, moving a string of a half-dozen mares through a gate to fresh grass, waved to Lee as she rode by. She returned their wave and forced a smile she hoped didn't look as artificial as it felt. She noticed that both had rifles in scabbards attached to their saddles and both wore holstered pistols.

The side arms seemed strange on the two cowboys. Ben's Colt and holster seemed to be almost a part of him—as natural-looking as his Stetson or his boots. But on the men guiding the mares, the guns seemed as out of place as a snapping turtle in a church-social punch bowl. Slick jigged a half step to the side to avoid the remains of a prairie dog killed by a coyote, and the movement of his body brought Lee's knee in light contact with the stock of the Winchester 30.06 in its scabbard rigged to her saddle.

It'd be crazy not to be armed after what happened. But as soon as those herds are gone, so are the guns from the Busted Thumb.

Several mares with foals at their sides ambled over to the fence line as Lee rode past. As docile as pussycats, the mares had known nothing but loving care, and their foals exhibited no fear at passersby.

Within twenty minutes, Lee had left the largest pastures behind and headed out to the far reaches of the ranch. The fences at the periphery—those encompassing pastures already grazed down and those that had been left fallow to be replanted—were Lee's concern this day.

The sun was high as Lee held Slick to a slow lope, riding a few feet inside the tightly strung smooth wire. A sharp glint ahead of her a hundred yards caught her eye. As she drew closer, the bit of light became many bits, looking like dew sparkling in the morning sun. She drew rein and dismounted.

What had been so pretty from a distance was a shattered whiskey bottle. The pieces of glass told her what had happened: Someone had put plenty of lead into the ground while shooting at the bottle. She ground tied Slick and walked the fence line, looking at the ground on the other side. What she thought was a long, twisted stick turned out to be a dead blacksnake, its thick body punctured dozens of times by bullets. *The farmer's friend,* she thought sadly. *No one but a drunk or a cruel misfit would kill a blacksnake.* Flies clustered about the corpse, and the sight of the slaughtered snake brought bile to the back of Lee's throat.

She was stepping into her stirrup when Slick's ears perked and pointed out to the open prairie. In a moment, she too heard the faint whoop. She mounted and listened intently. Faint laughter reached her, and then a series of pops—gunfire reduced by distance to little more than Chinese firecrackers.

Anger struck Lee like an unanticipated slap across the face. *Fools! They have no right to be shooting their guns like that! Suppose I had horses out here!*

The deeper, more throaty concussion of a heavy rifle sounded, and then sounded again. Slick danced under Lee, made skittish by the gunfire and by the tension his rider was transmitting.

The shouts were louder now, and the random shots clearer and closer. Lee heard the steady pounding of horses at speed. She swallowed hard and reached forward, drawing the 30.06 from its scabbard, working the lever to put a live round in the chamber. She placed the rifle across the saddle in front of her, just behind the horn, and put the index finger of her right hand inside the trigger guard. With her left hand holding the stock, she could swing the rifle into play in a heartbeat.

Three of the men topped a rise first. Their horses were in full gallop, and the rider in the middle was clutching a rifle. In half a moment, four others followed. The men reined in as if on signal and spread out in a ragged line.

Slick snorted a challenge to the other horses, but the fatigued mounts allowed it to go unanswered. Two of the men broke from the line and walked their horses to within a couple of feet of the fence line. Lee caught the flash of light on a bottle upturned to a man's mouth.

There were some mumbled words followed by braying laughter.

Lee turned Slick to face the two men head-on. Both were lean, unshaven, and dressed as cowhands. Both wore battered Stetsons that shaded their eyes. Both, Lee saw, carried pistols in holsters. The taller of the two, the one with the rifle, had a long, drooping mustache and sat lazily in his saddle, crooking his right leg around his saddle horn as if he'd stopped to chat with a neighbor. The other, a lump of tobacco tucked to the side of his mouth, spat a long, viscous stream of amber liquid to the side. More laughter erupted from the rest of the group.

"What's that big ol' rifle for, lil' lady?" the taller man asked. "You ain't up to no good now, are ya?"

"I have horses around here. You men have no right to be shooting."

"Well, lookit, honey," the tobacco chewer said, "why don't you go an' fetch yer husband, an' we'll talk to him about what we can an' can't do."

Sweat broke out on Lee's palms. "I'll ask you to ride back to wherever you came from and stay away from my land."

The rifleman guffawed, showing broken and yellowed teeth. "You'll *ask* us? Honey, I don't think you're in no position to ask us or tell us nothin'."

Lee hoped her voice wouldn't break—and it didn't. "I can use this rifle. If we have trouble, you go down first, and then the man next to you."

"Well, lookit this, boys! You're right prickly, ain't you, sweetie?" the rifleman mocked. He lifted his gun and motioned the men behind him to come forward.

The 30.06 was suddenly at Lee's shoulder. She fired over the tobacco chewer's head and worked the lever with a snap of her wrist. "You men stay back there, you hear me?" She swept the barrel of the Winchester slowly across the men on the other side of her fence.

The rider with the mustache held up his rifle to stop the men behind him. He tipped his Stetson back, and Lee could see the rest of his face. There was a fever in his eyes; they were like those of a captured hawk. She shivered and hoped no one noticed.

"Here's what we're gonna do, honey," he said, still grinning. "You gonna get down from that good horse an' walk away. This crowbait of mine's about shot. As part of our deal, I won't kill you an' I won't let my boys have at you. Sound fair?"

Lee shot him in the right shoulder. The impact of the heavy slug plucked him out of his saddle and left him sprawled in the dirt and scrub. In the briefest part of a second following the report of her rifle, Lee and Slick were in a headlong gallop away from the fence line. A slug whistled past, close enough for her to feel its heat on the side of her face. She leaned forward in the saddle and cut Slick into grindingly tight turns. Slick squealed and almost went down but then regained his footing. He shook his head as he ran, and a spatter of hot blood stung Lee's cheek. She leaned to the side and saw that a slug had cut a red, three-inch furrow along her mount's muzzle. If Slick had been half a step faster or if she hadn't jammed him into a skidding turn precisely when she did, the round would have killed him— or her.

More blood from Slick's wound whipped back at her. Without a thought—with no planning at all—she set Slick for a sliding stop and wheeled his body back over his haunches. His rear hooves gouged furrows into the

73

soil and left him pointed in the direction he'd been racing from a heartbeat ago.

Dust and grit hung in the air around them, and a clump of torn-up buffalo grass, wrenched from the dry soil by Slick's steel shoes, hadn't yet hit the ground when Lee ratcheted the lever of her rifle and fired toward the two riders about a hundred yards behind her. The men immediately separated from their side-by-side position and slowed their horses. They'd gotten through the fence, probably by dropping a couple of loops over a post and using their horses to drag it from the ground, but the return fire slowed them.

Lee tracked one of the men with her rifle, the sight at the end of the barrel leading the rider. She took a deep breath and began to exert pressure on the trigger. Her previous shots had been scattered and unaimed. This one wouldn't be.

The tiny dark metal post that was her front sight moved consistently with the pace of the horse. The cowboy was scribing a wide arc, and she led the animal's pace by perhaps an inch. Her finger tightened on the trigger, and then she fired toward the sky, tipping the weapon up at the last possible moment and then slamming it into the scabbard. Tears of anger and fear sprang from her eyes as she brought Slick around in a scrambling half circle and again asked him for all the speed he could give her.

There were no more shots from behind. What could have happened mere seconds ago made Lee's breath catch in her throat. There was no doubt in her mind that had she fired, the bullet would have taken the man down—punched a hole in his chest and ended his life. It was bad enough that she'd wounded one man. The fact that she'd been the slightest twitch of a finger from

74

snuffing out a human being's life scared her as much as the confrontation.

Lee galloped toward home, but not even her concern over Slick's wound could dislodge the image from her mind.

"So Lee come in with Slick's blood on her face an' across her chest, an' Maria, she scream, *'Dios mio!* Lee ees shot!' But it wass not so. Slick's muzzle weel carry a scar, but it wass no worse than a wire cut, really. He got a scrape on hees rear too, but it ees *nada*. I went out with a bunch of the boys, but we find nothin' but tracks an' the busted-down section of fence." Carlos took a long drink from his coffee mug and set it on Ben's desk.

Ben was pacing like a mountain cat in a cage. He hadn't spoken since Carlos began his story. For a long moment he continued pacing. Then he stopped in front of the weapon locker and wrenched open the door. He pulled a double-barreled twelve-gauge shotgun from the peg where it hung and dragged the drawer under the rifles and shotguns open, pulling it off its tracks and launching a hail of rifle, pistol, and shotgun ammunition into the air.

"See?" Carlos observed calmly. "Thees ees how Lee say you would act, no?"

"Never mind how I'm acting!" Ben snarled. "A bunch of boozed-up lunatics almost kill Lee on her own land, and you want me to be calm about it?" Dropping to his knees, he began stuffing ammunition into his pockets.

"I din't say nothin' 'bout bein' calm, *mi amigo*. You theenk I din't ride for blood today? Maria, she try to grab my horse's bridle so I no go. Lee, she wass screamin', 'No, Carlos!' An' I ride out like Satan wass at my heels, an' the boys, they follow. But there wass nothing, Ben.

75

An' I cannot know where these men come from—which of those herds—an' what can I do with one *pistola* and one rifle? Get my men keeled? So, I think, first I talk with Ben. He weel—"

Ben stood with the cut-down shotgun clutched in a death grip in his right hand. "Do what you want. I'm ridin' out." He turned and began toward the door to the cells and the back of the office, where Snorty was sheltered. Carlos was on his feet and in front of Ben much faster than one would think a man of his girth could move.

"Move, Carlos. I don't have time for this!"

Carlos's face became hard. "I never think I raise my han' to *mi amigo*, Ben Flood. Now I weel—'stead of carryin' you back over Snorty's saddle from a cattle camp with your life leakin' out of you!"

Ben lurched at Carlos, shoulder first, but the Mexican spun him away against the wall. Ben's right fist came up, and Carlos grabbed it with both hands, straining against Ben's fury. Their faces were mere inches apart, and their eyes locked in an almost physical battle. Sweat broke on both their faces as Carlos dropped his grip with one hand and used it to grab Ben's left arm. They strained against one another like a pair of draft horses in a pulling contest, their teeth bared, eyes aflame, every sinew and muscle flint-hard and stretched almost beyond endurance.

An eternity passed. Sweat was literally popping from their faces. Their shirts were soaked and sticking to their chests and arms. Their eyes were welded together, but the flames were diminishing.

Carlos winked slowly at Ben, the eyelid under his bushy, dripping brow closing slowly like the curtain falling in a theater, and said, "Thees gets old, no?"

"You . . . you betcha," Ben gasped. "On three, okay?"

"*Uno, dos, tres . . .*"

Collapsing into one another's arms, the two struggled to draw breath. Ben stumbled to his chair behind his desk and fell into it. Carlos lumbered to the chair he'd left to intercept his friend.

Ben grunted and extended his trembling right hand and arm over his desk. "*Mi amigo,*" he said.

Carlos grimaced as he leaned forward to shake the hand. "*Es verdad,*" he answered.

"Coffee?" Ben asked.

"*Sí.* But not the lamp oil you make here. We go to the café. Thees day, I buy."

Doc was at a table toward the rear of the café, alone. Bessie O'Keefe, daughter of Mike O'Keefe, the owner, was pushing a broom around the room in a desultory manner, and she smiled at Ben and Carlos as they walked in. "Coffee an' pie?" she asked.

"My treat today," Carlos said.

Doc looked up from the newspaper he was reading. "Careful nothing flies out of Carlos's pocket when he pays you, Bessie. It hasn't been opened since Noah built the ark." He grinned, waving the men over to his table. He sniffed the air as his friends sat. "You boys been wrestling hogs or something?"

"Somethin' like that, Doc," Ben answered.

After Bessie brought the coffee and pie and topped off Doc's mug, the conversation became serious as Carlos related what had taken place at the Busted Thumb.

"Lee's okay, though? And Slick too?" Doc asked.

"Yeah," Ben said. "Lee's awful upset but not hurt. Slick's fine."

77

Doc sipped his coffee. "Shot this boy clean out of his saddle, eh?"

Carlos nodded. "Ees a right shoulder wound. She say for me to tell you, case his friends bring heem in to be patched up."

"Won't happen," Doc said. "They'll get him drunk and then get the slug out of him and stitch him up with horsehair. If it was a through-and-through, they'll dump whiskey in the hole and clean it up a bit, and he'll be riding herd tomorrow." He looked at Ben. "You hear from the army or the other jurisdictions?"

Ben sighed. "No help, Doc. The bluecoats are tied up with Indian troubles, and the other lawmen are stretched as thin as I am."

"Bad situation," Doc said. "Could turn into a regular range war."

The word *war* created a spark in Ben's mind. He set down his fork. "You men remember Monte Krupp? The buffalo man I shot against in the long-gun competition at the festival a while back?"

"*Sí.* A leetle guy who don' stand no taller than Lee, right? Can shoot the hat offa flea at a mile with that big Sharps of hees, no?"

"That's the man. He and I go way back—to the war and before it. His brother's a judge up in Laredo, and he always knows where Monte is. If I can get Monte here—"

"He's just one man, Ben," Doc interrupted. "What can the two of you hope to do against a hundred or more of those cattlemen?"

"Krupp is a whole platoon of sharpshooters wrapped up in that little body of his. The man's got more fight and more smarts than a sack full of wildcats." Ben pushed away from the table and stood. "I'm gonna send

78

a wire right now. If Monte's brother can reach him, he'll come."

Doc and Carlos watched Ben hurry out of the café. "That Krupp is a strange one," Doc said. "He's the nicest fellow you could ever meet—but there's something inside him that chews at him."

Carlos considered for a moment. "He ain't the sort of hombre anyone knows well, I don' think. He's a buffalo hunter, but he's not *like* a buffalo hunter. Him an' Ben, they fought together in the war. Something *muy mal* happened with them at Gettysburg, but I don' know what it wass. Ben, he won' talk about it."

"What do you mean he's not like a buffalo hunter?"

"Well, you know. He talks good. He been to college. An' you know the buffalo men, they're peegs? Drunk an' crazy an' smell like a dead mule? Monte, he ees kinda quiet, an' he keeps heemself clean an' don' cuss or drink whiskey. Ben says he carry books with heem wherever he go." Carlos paused for moment. "Books without peectures, I mean. All words."

The scream echoed through the night with a tortured resonance that brought to mind the death cries of a timber wolf. Even the hard cases of the Long Snake camp shivered and didn't meet one another's eyes. There was a pause and then another bellow of pain.

"Can't we at least let him get drunk an' passed out, Atticus?" a cowhand asked. "The bullet's up under the bone an' it's plumb hard to get at."

Toole drew on his cigarette, exhaled a plume of smoke, and glared at the man across the fire from him. "No booze. Soon's the slug's outta him, I want him on a horse an' ridin' hard. He can't do that if he's drunk. An'

79

gag him. I'm right sick of his squallin'." He spat into the fire. "Bring them other lunkheads over here," he ordered.

Within a few moments, six men stood before Atticus Toole. The ramrod was quiet for a long moment, rolling another cigarette with deft fingers. He leaned forward, took a burning branch from the fire, lit his smoke, and tossed the branch into the flames. "You boys are ridin' out as soon as the slug's outta Arty, there." He nodded toward the chuck wagon, where three men held down the cowhand while the cook excavated a 30.06 bullet from his shoulder. "I can't take the chance the woman didn't see you fools."

The men stood in a ragged line, a couple of them shuffling their boots in the dust like penitent schoolboys. "But boss, she was fifty yards away!" one complained. "She didn't see nobody but Arty an' Zeke."

Toole met the speaker's eyes. The man had opened his mouth to say something else but closed it quickly enough so that his teeth clicked together.

"I tol' the whole useless lot of you I didn't want no trouble till I figured out jus' how I want to handle this pissant marshall. Ain't no legal way he can run us offa open prairie, but he can make trouble 'bout rustlin', murder, an' rape."

"We wasn't stealin' no horses, boss," one of the men said. "An' we didn't kill nobody. We was jist playin' a bit with the lady. Ain't no call for you to—"

Toole stood, his hands at his sides. "You tellin' me how to run my outfit, are you?"

"Nosir, I ain't. But me an' the others, we been with the Snake almost three years. We ain't no kids you hired on at the start of the drive. It ain't fair that—"

"I never said nothin' 'bout bein' fair. Like I said, you all ride out when Arty can sit a horse without fallin' off more'n a couple times a mile."

A lean cowhand with dark hair reaching well below his shoulders took a step forward. His Mexican spurs shone in the light of the fire. He wore a Colt in a polished holster that was tied low on his right leg so that his fingertips grazed the grips. "Lotsa herds an' lotsa jobs, Atticus. I got no problem with ridin' on. Thing is, we got money comin'. I figure we got a little extra due too, since you ain't lettin' us finish out the drive."

Toole shifted his left foot back six inches. "Well, I don't see it quite that way," he said. His voice was quiet, without threat. Even so, the men sitting on the ground near the fire and coffeepot scrambled out of the line of fire.

"See," Toole went on, "you boys didn't finish the drive. You got no money comin' from me. Now, how about gatherin' up your things so you're ready to pull outta my camp?"

"I want what I got comin' to me, Toole."

"Sure." Toole grinned. "Make your move."

The moment stretched out until the tension was shattered by a yowl and a string of curses from the Long Snake cook, working over the wounded cowboy. "He bit me!" the cook bellowed.

The long-haired cowhand's eyes flicked instinctively toward the yell for the briefest bit of a second. Before he could recover, two of Toole's slugs slammed into his chest. He took a stumbling step backward, and the hardness left his face and eyes. More than anything, he looked surprised. Then he toppled over, dead before he hit the ground.

Toole held his smoking pistol loosely at his side. "Anyone else?"

After a moment he holstered his weapon. "Plant him out on the prairie somewhere where he won't get dug up. Then take Arty and go."

The cook stomped up to Toole, a soiled bandana wrapped around his arm. "I'm finished with him," he ranted. "I ain't playin' doc no more. Arty up an' spit out the gag and jawed down on me like a cat on a rat! I'm all finished with that thankless jasper!"

A long moan issued from the chuck wagon, and a shirtless man, his chest and right side slick with sweat and blood, fell out of the back gate of the wagon. He hit the ground hard on his right shoulder and screeched in pain.

"Plant him with the other one," Toole said, drawing his pistol and taking aim. He shot the man again. "Git to it an' then mount up and ride." He turned to the rest of his men. "Now, I want some of you boys to go out an' bring the ramrods of the other drives back here with you. I don't care if you gotta drag 'em outta their blankets, hog-tie 'em, and drag 'em here. We gotta talk, and we gotta talk now. That tin-star marshall has some big ideas about movin' us on. It's 'bout time to show him who's boss."

Moonlight washed through the darkness in Lee's kitchen, putting sharp edges on her counter and the lines of the range and table. It was almost bright enough to read by, but she was too nervous to concentrate on the Bible opened before her next to a long-cold mug of coffee. A horse in the main barn snorted and was answered by another. Hooves shifted on the straw-covered wooden floors.

Lee sighed and stood from her chair. Sleep had refused to come earlier, and she doubted that it would now. She went to her bedroom, dressed quickly in her day clothes, and left the house.

Slick's stall was at the end of the barn, in the corner. Lee didn't bother with a lantern—the moon lit the barn adequately. A couple of horses nickered at her, and she stopped at their stalls to rub a muzzle or scratch behind an ear.

Slick was down in his stall, curled into the fresh straw with his front legs tucked up close to his body and his rear legs up to his stomach, like a sleeping fawn. A smile crossed her face. There was an incongruity in seeing a 1,200-pound stallion sleeping as Slick did. The instinct of most horses demanded that they sleep standing so that they could flee any predator or danger. Slick, fearless in his stallion arrogance, apparently had no concern about his vulnerability. His exhalations burbled softly from his nostrils, making the sounds of a sleeping child.

Lee snapped her fingers, and Slick's head was up instantaneously. He eased his front end up on his forelegs and pushed the rear of his body under himself and then upward. He shook loose straw from his coat and stepped to the gate of his stall. Lee rubbed the velvet smoothness of the stallion's muzzle, and her fingertips grazed the quickly healing scar. The flesh, still hairless, was firm and warm.

What a wonderful night for a ride, Lee thought. She pictured herself and Slick at a lope, reveling in the cool air and the soft beauty of the moon. *A magic night. But those herds . . .*

Lee snorted angrily, surprising both herself and her horse. Nights like this were what made all the work and sweat and worry of running a horse-breeding operation worthwhile. She smiled wryly and remembered her uncle telling her, *"If it isn't in his blood, there's no way on God's earth a man can raise horses successfully. And if he's in it for the money, he might as well try to train milk cows to sing opera."*

The same, she knew, applied to a woman raising horses. She turned away from Slick and walked to the tack room. When she returned, she was carrying her horse's bridle. She opened the gate, stepped into the stall, and slid the bit into Slick's mouth. She fit the ear piece carefully, making sure no hairs were trapped under it, set the noseband, and led the stallion out into the aisle to the front of the barn. She grabbed a handful of mane, bounced once on her feet, and dragged herself onto Slick's back.

Lee had spent almost as many hours riding bareback as she had in a saddle. As a young girl she'd generally been in too much of a hurry to bother saddling up. And her uncle had approved of her riding bareback, knowing that with nothing between her body and the horse, she'd learn how the animal's muscles worked and how the tiniest bit of leg pressure could elicit the exact movements the rider was asking for.

Slick danced a bit under Lee as she decided where her ride in the moonlight would take her. Her favorite place, she decided, would be perfect. Atop a gradual rise a couple of miles from her home was a small plateau that encompassed a small stand of desert pines, several large boulders, and a long, almost benchlike rock outcropping. In a sense, it was her "secret" place, although Ben had visited it, and Carlos and many of the ranch hands had ridden over or past it on their way to various pastures. But that didn't matter—it still felt enchanted to Lee. She turned Slick and with a light pressure of her legs, put him into a lope.

A man sitting on a dusky-colored horse watched from his vantage point to the side of the barn as the woman rode off. Getting on to the Busted Thumb had been ridiculously easy—he'd simply ridden in at a slow jog. He watched until he could no longer see the woman, and then he reached back into his saddlebag and pulled out a pint bottle of whiskey. He pulled the cork with his teeth, took a long pull, gasped, belched, and shoved the cork back into the neck of the bottle before putting it back in his saddlebag.

He jigged his horse toward the house and rode a quiet circuit around it, peeking in the windows from his vantage point on horseback. There wasn't much to see. A large book open on a table in the parlor caught his eye, as did a rifle standing stock-down next to the front door. On the side of the house, the man helped himself to another drink from his bottle and then rode around the building again. As his alcohol-numbed fingers attempted to slide the bottle back into his saddlebag, he dropped it silently to the soft grass without realizing his clumsiness.

There were only two doors—one in front and one in back, off the kitchen. The Mex's house was even smaller, all on one floor, also with two doors. Snoring that sounded like a logging chain being dragged through a tin pipe racketed out from what must have been the bedroom of the Mex place.

Satisfied, the man clucked his mount into a lope and headed off into the prairie.

Dew was beginning to settle as Slick picked his way down the slope, back toward the main part of the ranch. Tendrils of fog shifted about as the breeze toyed with them, making visibility more difficult than it had been at 2:00 A.M., a couple of hours ago.

"Miss Lee? That you?"

Lee jolted straight on Slick's back, peering around her as if awakened from a shallow nap.

"Over here, Miss Lee."

She recognized the familiar voice of Sy Younghans, one of her long-time, year-round hands. In a moment, Sy stepped through a curtain of ground fog and let Slick sniff him.

"Hi, Sy. Everything okay?"

"Everthin's nice an' quiet."

"That's the way we want it around here," Lee said with a smile. "You have a good night—what's left of it."

"Yes'm. An' you do the same."

5

Lee picked up her coffee mug from Ben's desk, sipped at it, grimaced, and set it back down. "So," she continued, "I sniffed the bottle, and it was whiskey. Not a single person on my ranch uses spirits, Ben. I make sure of it when a hand signs on with us, and Carlos keeps a close watch on even the boys we bring in at haying time."

A vein had begun to throb at Ben's left temple. He sat erect in his chair, as stiff-backed as a judge proclaiming a sentence. "This was two nights ago?"

Lee nodded. "I knew you'd be upset. I thought it could have been a drifter—a saddle bum passing through, or . . . I don't know. But today, Carlos said if I didn't tell you about it, then he was going to."

"Carlos has men watching the houses and barns at night now?"

"Yes. He's got half the men working during the day and the other half riding all night. It's fairly slow at the ranch now, and only the general maintenance needs to be done. But when foaling starts, I'll need the help during the day. We'll be moving mares and the—"

"This'll be over long before foaling. I guarantee you that."

Lee reached toward her coffee, reconsidered, and dropped her hand to her lap. "Why would the herders be interested in my house or Carlos and Maria's? We checked carefully—there was nothing at all missing from the houses or the barns, not a hoofpick or a flake of hay. Certainly not a saddle or anything like that. And all the horses are accounted for."

"That bothers me even more," Ben said. "If this fellow wasn't there to steal, he was there for another reason."

"Like what?"

"I'm not sure. But that man wasn't out for a pleasure ride. He was there for a purpose. Look, I want one of your boys sleepin' downstairs in your house at night."

Lee's immediate impulse was to laugh, but she kept her mouth closed and her face immobile. She was glad she'd done so when she saw the concern in Ben's eyes. "I don't think that's necessary. I'm well armed, and if it makes you feel better, I'll bring the rifle by my door up to my bedroom with me at night."

Ben didn't respond for a moment. "Please don't argue with me on this," he finally said. "I'll swing by whenever I can at night. I'll identify myself by whistlin' . . . ummm . . . 'Buffalo Gals,' so Carlos and the others don't use me for a target."

"'Swing by?' It's a long ride each way, Ben—even on Snorty. You've got enough to tend to. You need your sleep. You're only one man and—"

"Not no more, I'm not," Ben said. "I wired Monte Krupp's brother—the judge—a couple days ago, lookin' for Monte. As luck would have it, Monte was there. That good buckskin horse, Daisy, twisted a leg steppin' into a prairie-dog hole, and he was waitin' out her healin' and spendin' some time with his brother and family. He'll be here some time today."

"Did he borrow a horse from his brother?"

"Nothin' but draft animals there. He'll rent a mount at Howard's livery when he gets in. He's takin' the stage here."

Lee smiled. "It's hard for me to imagine a man like Monte hunting buffalo. He sure isn't the type."

Ben nodded. "The way he told it to me was that he had to give it up after the war. He said he was all set up on a big stand an' ready to start shootin', and somethin' told him it was wrong—that there'd been enough slaughter, enough killin' in the world. He said he didn't question whatever it was that moved him that day. Guns are a kind of necessary evil, but he won't ever use a weapon for profit again."

"He's a good man." She laughed. "And can he eat! Remember when Maria put on that spread the last time he was here? He ate everything but the tablecloth, and then he was snooping in the kitchen not an hour later for the last piece of peach pie."

"That's Monte. If I ate like he does, I'd weigh more than Snorty."

Lee stood, smiling. "That you would. Well, I've got to get back to the ranch."

Ben stood up too. "Please, Lee, do what I asked. About havin' a man downstairs at night?"

"Oh, all right. I don't see the need of it, but if it'll make you feel better, okay."

Ben got up and walked around his desk to her. "Thanks, honey. It's important to me." He took her hand. "Don't forget to have Carlos let the men know I'll be stoppin' by at night from time to time—whistlin' 'Buffalo Gals.'"

"That'll be hard to miss, Ben. You whistle about as well as you sing."

A blonde woman stepped down from the passenger compartment of the West Texas Line stage onto the main street of Burnt Rock. In a moment a man followed. He was perhaps 5'7", lean, and dressed like a banker or merchant on a holiday. His dark suit fit him too well to have been purchased from a catalog or a general store, and his low boots with standard rather than riding heels were polished so that they reflected the sun in shards of gleaming light. He looked fresh-pressed and cool despite the heat and the hours spent in a dusty passenger compartment. He carried a leather valise in his left hand and a four-and-a-half-foot-long item rolled in a tanned square of buffalo hide in his right. He leaned the parcel against the stage and reached back inside to pick up a black bowler hat, which he centered neatly on his well-barbered, dark brown hair. Then he turned to assist the lady in receiving her suitcase from atop the stage.

A farm wagon driven by a man in overalls clattered up behind the stage. What appeared to be almost a dozen towheaded youngsters piled off the back of the flatbed and raced to their mother. She swept as many of the kids as she could into a loving hug, kissing them and fussing with them.

The well-dressed fellow picked up the long parcel and rested it over his shoulder. "Mrs. Kreiger," he said,

90

"thank you for making a tedious trip seem shorter. I've enjoyed our conversation thoroughly."

The woman looked up from her swarm of children. "I enjoyed it too, Mr. Krupp. Good luck with your business here."

Monte nodded and turned away to set off down the street. His stride was long, and he walked with his back straight, like a soldier being watched on the drill field by a superior officer.

Ben stood waiting at his office door as his friend approached. Monte dropped his valise to the floor, placed the parcel on Ben's desk, and held out his right hand.

"Ben," he said, smiling, "it's been too long."

Ben took his friend's hand. "That's for sure, Monte. Much too long. Good to see you—an' sorry about Daisy too. How's she doin'?"

"She's coming along fine. Another week or ten days and they'll take the wrap off her leg and start to exercise her, and she'll be as good as new."

The two men stood grinning at one another for a moment, hands still together between them.

Ben broke the silence. "How about some coffee?"

"I thought you'd never ask. But not that slop you make, Ben. Let's go down to the café where we ate when I was last in Burnt Rock—where that pretty Bessie bakes those wonderful pies. I'm near starved."

Ben started to the door. "Fine with me," he said. "You never did appreciate fine coffee, anyway."

"Wait," Monte said. "Give me a moment to check my gear." He began to untie the latigo strings around his parcel. "I carried it with me in the coach, but a man can never be too careful about his equipment, can he?"

Monte rolled out the buffalo hide, revealing a long rifle with an octagonal barrel. The stock was of highly polished cherry wood, and the blued steel of the barrel, trigger assembly, and cocking lever glistened with a light coating of gun oil. A short, adjustable-height tripod was tucked into a pocket of the hide, where its metal frame couldn't touch any part of the rifle.

"That's a new barrel," Monte said. "I had the entire rifle refitted by the Sharps Company, out there in Hartford, Connecticut. It's a 1.10 caliber now—takes a 110-grain cartridge that'll shoot darn near to the moon without losing a hair of accuracy."

Ben began to reach for the rifle but stopped mid-motion and looked at Monte. Monte nodded. "Go ahead. Pick her up."

Ben lifted the buffalo gun from the hide and held the butt to his shoulder. "Seems heavier," he observed.

"About sixteen pounds since the refit," Monte said. "Don't forget, that's a thirty-four-inch barrel. The 1851 model only had the thirty-inch barrel. That accounts for some weight. Plus, the heavier chamber adds some too."

Ben worked the lever. "Whew! That's the smoothest action I've ever felt. Fine weapon, Monte. Real fine."

Monte smiled proudly. "It gets the job done in good order. Now—about that coffee and pie . . ."

O'Keefe's Café was in the midst of its afternoon lull when Ben and Monte walked in. Mike O'Keefe was sitting at a front table, smoking his pipe and reading a newspaper. He nodded at Ben and then smiled broadly at Monte.

"Good to see you again, Monte. I didn't know you were in town."

"Same to you, Mike. I didn't know I'd be here until a few days ago. Bessie is well, I hope?"

"Fit as a fiddle. She's out in back. You boys set at a table, an' I'll send her on out."

"I didn't know you knew the O'Keefes that well, Monte," Ben observed as they headed by unspoken assent to the rear table.

"Last time I was here, Bessie and I attended the stage play that traveling troupe put on."

Ben raised his eyebrows. "Funny, I didn't hear nothin' about that."

"There were posters all over the place. I don't see how you could have—"

"Not about the play—about you takin' Bessie to see it. You didn't say anything."

"I had to leave Burnt Rock the next morning. We thought we'd see you and Lee there."

Ben felt his face redden as he pulled out a chair so that his back would be to the wall. "Well . . . Lee mentioned the play. The thing is, there was a herd at the stockyards, an' they had a kid there—a roper—who was real good. Carlos had a fellow workin' for him who could catch an' tie a calf 'fore a frog could croak. We kinda set up a little contest, an' I pure forgot about the play."

Monte smiled. "Carlos's boy win?"

It was Ben's turn to grin. "Carlos an' me got treated to coffee an' pie by the ramrod. His roper missed two loops on ten head of cattle."

"That must have pleased Lee no end," Monte said. "I'll be sure to mention it when I see her. Of course, you told her you were out gawking at cowboys rather than taking her to the play, right?"

"Do that an' you'll find that fancy Sharps of yours at the bottom of a rain barrel."

Monte shook his head. "Sorry, Ben. If that fine lady's spending time with a profligate who doesn't even—"

93

Bessie's rush to the table ended the discussion. "Monte, what a grand surprise! I had no idea you were coming."

Monte stood and shook Bessie's hand. It seemed to Ben that either Bessie or Monte extended the touch of their hands a bit longer than necessary. Just then, Doc walked in the front door of the café, and Ben waved him back to their table.

"We'll continue our conversation later, all right, Bessie?" Monte said.

"Sure." Bessie waited until Doc was seated. "What'll it be, gentlemen?" she asked. "I have fresh apple pie."

"That sounds great," Monte said. "But first, I need a beefsteak about the size of this table, a bowl of your mashed potatoes, and lots of coffee."

"There goes my budget for the month," Ben groaned. "You might as well put Doc's pie an' coffee on my tab too—an' I'll have an extra big slice myself, with coffee."

"All right, I'll get that for you right away," Bessie said and headed back to the kitchen.

"Good to see you, Monte," Doc said, reaching across the table to shake hands. "You keeping well?"

"I'm just fine," Monte answered. "You too, Doc?"

"Great." Doc paused. "I wish you were here on a social visit, Monte. I already have my chessboard out. But we've got a real big problem."

"Then maybe you boys better fill me in," Monte said. His eyes met Ben's. "I don't know what you're up against here. But you know you've got all the help I can give you."

"I know that. And I'm grateful to you," Ben said. He sighed. "Here's what's happening . . ."

Monte Krupp listened attentively, asking a few questions and sipping at his coffee after Bessie had served it. Doc added a few comments and reiterated the story about the gored cowboy on Main Street.

The three men were quiet as Bessie served Monte's meal. She must've noticed the change in the texture of the conversation, because she left the men to eat and talk, telling them to yell out if they needed more pie, coffee, or anything else.

Monte ate in silence for a few moments. "I know of Atticus Toole," he finally said. "He's a bad actor from way back. Rode with a couple of the gangs right after the war. Meaner than a scorpion in a brush fire, is what I've heard."

Doc nodded. "That's what folks say. It seems like his type—and the men who ride with him—understand and respect only one thing: strength and violence. And even given your skills, Monte, you and Ben are only a pair of men against maybe a hundred cutthroats and hard cases."

"Too bad the army couldn't help out," Monte said.

"It is, but they're spread awfully thin these days. But even beyond the danger from the cattlemen, I think we're missing the main point here," Doc said. "Those longhorns out there on the prairie are a powder keg. If something spooks them and puts a real stampede into motion, the natural slope of the land will bring them right through Burnt Rock."

"Not through, Doc," Monte said. "Over. With that many of them in a blind panic and running hard, they'd shred everything standing in their way, including buildings and people. I saw a decent-sized herd of buffalo plow through a little mining town back in '69. You'd think God had decided to level the place if you'd seen the wreckage and carnage afterward. Good stout structures—a few stores, a saloon, a church—were nothing but kindling. The miners' tents and shanties were crushed into the ground, along with the men in them."

"What started the rush?" Doc asked. "Gunfire? Thunder?"

"Hard to say. It's not so much thunder that'd set them off, but the lightning. That spooks them. I imagine the longhorns we're talking about have heard about as much gunfire as the boys at Gettysburg did. But it's impossible to predict what'll start a stampede. I've seen a pair of buffalo bulls fighting over mating rights to a cow start a major run. Other days the bulls could fight until one of them drops dead, and the herd wouldn't pay any more attention to them than they would a prairie dog."

A dark silence settled over the table. After a moment, Ben said, "Seems to me that there's not much we can do about the cattle. It's the herders we gotta get rid of. And the only way to get them to move on is to use what they understand against them."

"Agreed," Monte said. "Even those fellows don't have any trouble figuring out a lead slug means trouble."

Doc shook his head slowly. "I don't doubt that you boys are right. It's times like this, though, when what ol' Rev Tucker used to say comes to mind: Violence begets violence."

Ben rode at a walk toward the ramshackle camp of the Long Snake Cattle Company. The sun had barely poked above the horizon, and faint wraiths of smoke rose from the small fires scattered near the massive herds of longhorns. Snorty sniffed the air and shook his head, again nervous about the huge horde of snorting, bawling creatures. Ben held a tight rein, feeling his mount's apprehension.

Thicker, more visible smoke rose from the fire pit to the rear of the chuck wagon, where the morning meal was well underway. Shuffling about, the cowboys rubbed sleep from their eyes or drank coffee from thick ceramic mugs. A few sat on the ground, rolling cigarettes. The night guards were shagging their weary horses into the remuda—the small herd of horses needed to keep so many men mounted on fresh stock daily—while a few of the just-awakened men were selecting their horses for the day, dropping large loops over the animals' heads and leading them away to be saddled and bridled.

Ben knew his approach had long since been conveyed to Atticus Toole by the sentries who rode the periphery of the herd. Eyes swung toward him as he rode past clusters of men drifting toward the chuck wagon. He heard some mumbled curses but didn't respond.

Toole strode out toward him, a shotgun resting over his shoulder. Ben reined in, and Toole stopped twenty feet or so in front of the cook's wagon.

"You got some business here?" he asked.

"Plenty. You've got five days to buy what supplies you need, get your cattle together, and move out."

Toole spat on the ground in front of Snorty. His smile was mocking. "Seems like I heard somethin' jus' like that not too long ago. I'm still here, my cattle are still here, and so are the other herds."

"Somethin' else too," Ben said. "The ranches around here are off limits to any of you herders. A bunch of your riders upset a lady, shot at her, marked her horse. One of you was pokin' around the Busted Thumb a couple days ago in the middle of the night. Next one who tries that will be brought back here tied over his saddle like a sack of grain."

Toole spat again. "This is gettin' right boring, Flood. Las' time, I asked you if you an' your fat Mex deputy was gonna run all of us out. I got the same question today."

"I'm thinkin' you've got a cowhand with a rifle wound in his shoulder," Ben said, ignoring Toole's question. "That man's under arrest. Where is he?"

Toole's laugh was like a sharp bark of a dog. "I got no wounded men. An' you actually think you could arrest one of 'em here in this camp? You're dreamin', Flood. Pure dreamin'."

"Like I said, you've got five days, starting tomorrow. You'd best get your operation in order and set to move."

"You can't force us to go nowhere. You're one man with a tin star—an ol' dog with no teeth. Ride out while I'm still of a mind to let you go."

Ben was silent for a moment. Then he removed his Stetson, wiped his forehead with his sleeve, and resettled his hat on his head.

The galvanized, three-gallon coffeepot suspended by its handle over the cook fire suddenly spewed a wave of boiling coffee and grounds into the fire and around it. A jagged, fist-sized hole had appeared in the pot almost a full second before a ponderous burst of thunderlike racket rolled through the camp. Toole spun to gawk at the pot.

A lantern hanging at the top of the chuck wagon erupted a sheet of burning fuel that engulfed the canvas in flames, and in a moment, the booming, thunderous report tolled again. The cook fire exploded like a volcano, hurtling burning wood, white-hot embers, and fiery coals into the air. A cauldron full of stew next to the burning wagon leaped into the air, spinning crazily, disgorging potatoes, chunks of raw beef, pound after

98

dripping pound of beans, and a bunch of onions in a wide swath.

The very earth trembled with the concussive pounding. Toole, swinging his shotgun toward Ben, was thrown backward by an explosion between his feet and slammed into a cowhand, leaving them both on the ground in a tangle of arms and legs.

The thunder stopped. "Toole!" Ben bellowed. "Five days!" Then he wheeled Snorty and let his horse run.

About three-quarters of a mile away, atop a gentle rise, Monte Krupp sat on a wide-eyed, heavily sweated rental horse from the Burnt Rock livery stables. Monte's Sharps and tripod were already wrapped in the buffalo skin, and the latigo was tied securely at each end. He carried the rifle across his lap, secured by his right hand. His left hand held tight reins against the dancing, plunging horse under him. Ben loped up and stopped.

"The horse didn't much care for the shooting?" he asked.

"Good thing we brought the hobbles. He was leaping up and down like a sunstruck jackrabbit. He's none the worse for it, though. A tad nervous, is all. He'll calm down on the way back to town."

Ben grinned. "Real fine shooting, Monte."

Monte nodded and smiled back. "That's what I'm here for, my friend."

Toole's camp looked like it had been under a three-day siege. Cowhands scrambled about, trying to contain the fires in the chuck wagon and the supply wagon, while others stamped out the tongues of flame that had spread out from the main fires into the grass and scrub.

Toole cursed and launched a kick at the wreckage of the coffeepot. The side the soft-nosed slug had gone into was punctured with a fist-sized hole. The exit opening was four times that size, with spirelike fingers of twisted metal pointing outward.

"Was one of them Sharps carbines," he growled. "Ain't nothin' else shoots a slug that big or sounds like this one did." He spun to holler at the men. "An' you lily-livered cowards didn't even shoot back! One man had you runnin' an' dodgin' like ya never heard gunfire before! What kind of a bunch of women are you? Why didn't you shoot back?"

"Uhh . . . wasn't nobody to shoot at, boss. We couldn't even tell where the shots was comin' from," one of the hands answered.

"Then why didn't you gun Flood? He was settin' there grinnin' big as a barn! Somebody shoulda dropped him dead!"

"Kinda thought you'd do that, boss."

Toole cursed again. "Get them fires out! When that's done, I want each of the ramrods from the other herds here before high noon. That lawman is lookin' for a fight, an' I'll tell you what—that's what he's gonna git!"

Monte stood in front of the livery barn, his eyes sweeping the length of Main Street. Two boys riding bareback on a rolling-fat old draft horse with bamboo fishing poles over their shoulders jogged past, a spotted dog frolicking at their side. The town was quiet—even the out-of-tune piano at the Drovers' Inn was blessedly still—and there was little pedestrian traffic. Two old fellows sat on a bench in front of Scott's Mercantile, each turned to the checkerboard between them. A pair of ranchers stepped out of O'Keefe's Café and stopped by their horses at the hitching rail. One laughed at something the other said and tossed his arm affectionately over his friend's shoulder. Monte headed that way, hoping a few words with Bessie and a cup of coffee would change the focus of his thoughts.

He knew a large herd of cattle was, in a very real sense, a single, living thing. Each of the members of the herd was born with needs and fears and instincts given them by their Creator. But when the animals gathered together in great numbers, each of their instincts became as one governing unit. The problem was that the leader need not be the strongest or the fastest or the bravest animal, but rather that one which acted or reacted first. The others, in their mindless and unthinking numbers, would follow that leader, be it a cow or bull or steer.

Longhorns were the easiest type of cattle to raise on sparse grazing, poor water, or in foul weather. The bulls were huge creatures, often weighing 1,200 pounds or more, and their horns frequently measured five feet from tip to tip. They were hardy animals—Monte had once heard an old herder say, "A longhorn can gain five pounds a day eating rocks and drinking sand."

But he knew the word *easy* needed to be qualified. Longhorns could be turned out to pasture and left essentially alone to graze and roam until it was time to bring them into a herd and move them to boxcars. That was when they earned their reputation as being the quickest, meanest, most bloodthirsty animals on the face of the earth. Monte knew that savvy, well-trained cow horses were lost every year to the sharply tapered spikes at the ends of horns that were as thick as a powerful man's wrist. The raw mass and destructive capability of a running bull was like that of a high-balling locomotive; it could shatter or shred anything or anyone standing in its path.

Perhaps *intelligence* was too human a word to apply to longhorn cattle. The animals were guided only by instinct, but that instinct often appeared to be cunning in the perception of humans. He believed it was true that some creatures—dogs, horses, cats—could love. But longhorns couldn't. Their only aims were to stay alive, to protect themselves, and to eat, sleep, fight or run, and reproduce. Anyone or anything that prevented a longhorn from doing any of those things could get hurt—or worse.

And Monte knew from experience that there was one universal sensation or emotion longhorns could feel: panic.

Bessie O'Keefe's eyes sparkled like those of a child on Christmas morning. "Oh, Lee," she gushed, "I'm not even sure why I rode out here. I know you're busy with your ranch and all, and you've got all those horses to look after, but I'm just bursting with good news, and I didn't know where else to go!"

"Hush now, Bessie! I'm happy to see you, and my work's done for the day. Don't you dare say another word about taking up my time. I don't get to see you to chat except after church or at the café, and even then there's not enough time to really talk with one another. Here, let me get you some coffee." She moved to the stove, brought the coffeepot to her kitchen table, and poured some into a couple of mugs. "I'm sorry I don't have any pie or cake to offer you. I love to bake sweets, but the only time I have the time it takes is during the winter."

"Ugh!" Bessie exclaimed. "If you had to bake cakes an' pies every morning before the sun's up, you'd soon find that it loses its charm."

"Probably so," Lee agreed. "It's a luxury to me, but it's a matter of business to you and Mike. But you enjoy the café, don't you?"

"Oh, sure. My pa makes lots of noise, but he's a pussycat to work for, and he really appreciates what I do. And I love the folks who come in every day—Ben and Doc and Missy and Mr. Scott from the mercantile . . . and all the rest of them. The money is good too. Pa insists on paying me what a restaurant manager and cook would get in a bigger town."

"But you were talking about possibly going off to nursing school a couple years back, weren't you?"

Bessie sipped her coffee before answering. "Well, yes, I was. I'd written the application and sent it off, and I was accepted. Then when the time to go got closer and closer, and I thought more about it, I decided that it wasn't for me. I'm a small-town girl, and leaving Burnt Rock and our church and all the people I know—well, I simply couldn't do it. So I didn't."

"Do you sometimes wish you'd gone off to the school, though, just to see what it would be like?"

"Oh, once in a while, I guess. 'Least I did before last night, anyway. Now things are all different."

Lee raised her eyebrows. "Different? How so?"

Bessie's eyes shone even more brightly, and a fetching blush moved into her cheeks. "'Cause . . . 'cause I have a beau now, Lee! And there was just nobody to tell in town except old ladies and little kids, so I saddled up right after dinner and rode out here to tell you."

"Why, that's wonderful, Bessie! A sweet girl like you deserves to be married and have a family. Who's the lucky man?"

"It's Monte Krupp! Remember when he was here about eight months ago? Well, all during that time we were seeing each other. We didn't want the town to find out, 'cause you know how that is—there'd be nothing but gossip and teasing. We wrote back and forth when Monte was gone, and last night he said he loved me and wanted me to be his wife! Isn't that glorious?"

Lee struggled not to let her shock show on her face. "That's really . . . uhh . . ."

Bessie laughed delightedly. "I know just what you're thinking, Lee Morgan. Monte is twenty years older than I am. Well, we discussed that, and we just don't give a hoot!"

Lee waited for a moment before speaking, marshalling her thoughts. Her voice was soft when she spoke. "It's not the age difference I'm concerned about, Bessie. The thing is, Mr. Krupp's not a Christian. He's a fine man, and he has all sorts of good qualities, but it seems to me that, well . . ."

Bessie laughed again and rushed around the table to hug Lee. "That's the best part of all! He is a Christian—he committed his life to Jesus six months ago in Tucson!"

"Are . . . are you absolutely sure of all this, Bessie? Are you positive that what Mr. Krupp said is—"

"I *do* know it's true! I've prayed about it, and I know what my heart tells me and what the Lord tells me. I want you to be happy for me. Can't you do that?"

For the moment, Lee forced down her doubts. "Of course, I can. And I am. It's just such a huge surprise . . . my friend Bessie's going to be a bride!"

Lee held Bessie close for a long moment. *What do I really know about Monte Krupp?* she wondered. *There's a strange and powerful bond between Ben and him—and it has something to do with the war they fought in together. Ben won't—or can't—talk about those days, but isn't his love for Monte a testament to the man's character?*

The women eased out of their embrace. There were tears of happiness on Bessie's cheeks. "I'll ask that you keep all this between us for now, Lee. I was just busting out to share it all with someone. I haven't even told my pa yet. Give me your word you'll keep hush for a bit, all right?"

"Of course, I will. Now, I know baking time comes awfully early at O'Keefe's Café. I'm going to rustle up one of my men to ride back to town with you. I saw Sy Younghans a few moments ago, and I know he has tomorrow off. I'm sure he'll go along with you."

"Oh, don't be silly! I'll be fine. I'll—"

"Absolutely not," Lee insisted. "You're not riding alone in the dark all that way with everything that's been going on." She forced her face into a hard scowl. "I'm not missing out on a wedding reception put on by Mike O'Keefe, young lady!"

6

Monte leaned over Ben's desk and drew on the blank side of a wanted poster. "See what I mean?" he asked without looking up. "It doesn't have to be a moat. All we need is a trench maybe four feet deep, all the way around the town."

"Whew," Ben breathed. "You ever try to dig in that dirt? I still have calluses on my hands an' a crick in my back from when we dug the foundation for the church."

Monte sat back in his chair. "Oh," he said sarcastically. "I forget about your lily-white hands, Ben. Sorry. Let's just sit back and watch Burnt Rock be leveled."

"You know it ain't the work stoppin' me. The thing is, I don't think I'll be able to sell the idea to the town." He paused for a moment. "An' to tell you the truth, I can't say I'm 100 percent convinced it's necessary. I've heard about stampedes, and I don't doubt those longhorns would tear up the town a bit if they got to running. But if a run does start, we'll get the folks into the biggest buildings in town—the hotel an' Scott's Mercantile—an' wait it out. You can't tell me that those cattle will breach buildings set on solid foundations and built around rough-cut beams a foot and a half thick. Why—"

"That's precisely what I *am* telling you!" Monte stood quickly, leaning toward Ben. "You've never seen what a thousand-pound animal can do in a panic. They're like cannonballs—nothing will stop them until they drop from exhaustion. Multiply what one can do times the three thousand or better longhorns out there, and I'll tell you what—your town will be kindling, and you'll have a whole lot more digging to do than a simple trench!"

Ben held up his hands. "Sit down, Monte—and calm down. Look, Toole's men have been coming in for supplies, an' so have Harmon Kenny's boys from the Double D. A slew of the X2 and Tall Hill wagons came in yesterday. They're all buyin' staples: flour, coffee, salt, beans, sugar, canned fruit."

Monte sat back down. "And ammunition, Ben. I talked to Mr. Scott last night. The herders bought his full supply of 30.30 and 30.06 ammo and put a big dent in his .45 and .38 stock."

"I hadn't heard that," Ben said. "Could be they're just replenishing supplies. Although . . ."

"Right. It doesn't make a bit of sense. Buy all that firepower to go down the prairie a couple hundred miles or so and then haul the provisions all the way back to where the herds started from? You know as well as I do that the cowhands hired on for a drive are cut loose at its end, and that the wagons go back almost empty, except for what the permanent help and the cook need to get them home."

Monte stood again and walked toward the coffeepot on Ben's potbellied stove, mug in hand. When he spoke, his voice was controlled but there was strong emotion behind it. "You can't think my little shooting display two days ago scared off Toole and the others, Ben." He stopped halfway to the stove and turned to face his friend. "That's a rough bunch. They've seen fancy shooting before. We caught them when they were hungover, asleep, and suspecting nothing. That won't happen again."

"I don't think we scared them off. But I think we showed them some of what they'll face if they're not gone in three days. In their hearts, those men are cowards. They wouldn't live the lives they do if they could make it on their own without their gang around them."

"You don't understand my point," Monte protested. "It's not the men I'm worried about, it's the herds and the threat of a stampede." He shook his head in exasperation and walked back to his chair, setting his still-empty mug on Ben's desk. "If I have to make my point to the entire town, then that's what I'll do." He paused. "How about this: If the herds aren't gone in two days—that'll make it Sunday—how about if I talk to the folks at church? I'll go over to the newspaper office and have some half sheets printed up inviting the whole town to hear what I have to say. After they hear me, it's up to them. Fair enough?"

Ben considered for a moment. "Sounds fair enough to me. Yeah, sure."

Monte sighed. "Good." He glanced at his coffee mug. "Let's go over to the café and get some decent coffee. Yours tastes like you boiled a sackful of cactus in the pot."

"Seems like you spend lots of time at the café, Monte," Ben said with a grin. "I'm wondering if Bessie has anythin' to do with that."

Monte pondered the question. "Well," he said, "it could be that your coffee's so rank it'd kill a scorpion if he stepped in a drop of it. But the fact of the matter is that it *is* Bessie. You see, my friend, I'm going to marry her."

The office door swung open—hard. Carlos, his face grim and his eyes slightly squinting, stepped in from the bright sunlight of Main Street. "There ees bad trouble, Ben. Sy Younghans was shot dead last night, an' Bessie O'Keefe, she ees missing. She din't come home last night—Mike has no seen her. She never—"

"What?" Monte barked. "Bessie is missing?"

"*Sí.*" Carlos's eyes shifted between Ben and Monte as he spoke. "She rode out an' visited with Lee las' night. Lee send Sy to ride with her to home. Sy's mare, she come back an' wass standin' outside the barn when I got up thees morning. I backtracked her an' found Sy. Wass three, maybe four riders, who take Bessie. I follow them to the Dos Gatos an' then los' the trail an' come here."

"Carlos," Ben said, "you better go to the livery and fetch a fresh horse. Happy has to be done in by now. Monte, you ready to ride?"

"Not quite," Monte said. "I'll be back in a couple of minutes."

Carlos looked questioningly at Ben and nodded toward the Sharps leaning in the corner. "That ees Monte's buffalo gun, no? What does he need?"

"Did you see his eyes, Carlos? I've seen Monte like this a few times before, during the war. Our best bet is to let him be."

"I dunno what you're saying. Why ees he . . . ?"

"Monte just finished tellin' me he and Bessie are gonna be married."

110

"Dios mio," Carlos breathed. "These men who took Bessie—they weel soon be dead, no?"

"Go get a horse. I'll saddle Snorty."

Monte was vaguely aware of the hotel clerk greeting him as he entered the building. He didn't respond; the man's presence barely registered in his brain. His mind was forming and planning his next few hours.

Monte unlocked his room and strode to his dresser. He opened the top drawer and removed a folded leather pouch. In it were two Swedish-steel-bladed knives with flat ivory grips. Each of the knives had an odd, scimitarlike hook at the end of its six-inch blade. He took his handkerchief from his pocket and carefully wiped the light oil from each of the knives and inserted them into the sheaths sewn inside his boots.

His handguns were in the bottom drawer. He took off his coat and strapped on the dual holster affair by putting his arms through narrow belts that ran over his shoulders. The bone grips of a pair of Colt .45s pointed forward about five inches below each armpit. He drew each weapon and checked their loads—five rounds in the cylinders with the hammers resting on the empty. He spun the cylinder on each Colt with his thumbs, and the sound was that of an oiled, barely audible hum.

As he shrugged into his coat and turned to leave the room, his eyes fell on his Bible, open on the small table next to the bed. He walked over and picked it up. The cover smelled of leather, and the pages were a pristine white, the text crisp and starkly black like a flock of crows on fresh snow. Monte stood for several minutes, holding the book before he spoke aloud. "Bessie is as pure as this Bible, Lord. I ask your help in finding her and keeping her safe." He closed the Bible gently and placed it on the table. Then he turned and walked to the door.

"They went into the water here," Ben said.

Monte dismounted and hunkered down at the shore. While touching a hoofprint, he said, "Looks like this horse was being led by the rider in front of it."

"That's what I figured," Carlos said. "I crossed here an' rode four, maybe five mile an' din't see no more tracks. The river starts into a valley, an' there's too much cover. If these riders, they left a man behind, he'd have a fine shot at me, no? So I rode to town. I ain' no good on a search if I'm dead."

"You did the right thing, Carlos," Ben said.

Monte stood up. "You went back to Lee's ranch first off, right? After you backtracked Sy's horse?"

"Sí. I knew nothing of Bessie. I put Sy over my saddle an' took heem to the Thumb, an' Lee tol' me she wass ridin' with him. I saw there were two horses when I tracked Sy's mare, but I theenk to myself he was ridin' with another wrangler, an' maybe that man wass hurt somewheres too."

Ben stepped down from Snorty. "You've got to get to the Busted Thumb," he said to Carlos. "I know you've got good men there, but they need you to lead them if anythin' else happens." After a moment he added, "And Maria and Lee are there."

Carlos wiped the sweat from his forehead with his sleeve. "I know thees ees true. But Monte, my heart wants to ride with you. Ben tol' me about you an' Bessie. She ees a fine woman. All the time she have the smile for me. All the time she ask after my grandson, an' she send a pie with Maria to me." His voice began to break. "Now I can no even . . ."

Monte strode over to Carlos and extended his right hand. "There isn't another man on earth I'd rather have with me than you and Ben. And I know about responsibility too. Go on—go and keep those women and that ranch safe."

Carlos took Monte's hand and shook it. Then, wordlessly, he spun his horse and rode off at a fast lope.

"A good man," Monte said.

"He is that. Now, what's your plan?"

"Isn't but one way to do this that I can see," Monte answered. "Ride down the river—in the river, as much as I can, to keep the noise down—find where these men have Bessie, kill them, and take Bessie home. It's simple, really. After that, move on the herders."

"You've got to think about strategy, Monte. This was a good move on their part."

"Yeah. They think they have a lever now. They settle in, and if we start picking them off, they use Bessie as a bargaining chip. If we don't leave them be, they kill her."

Ben stepped into a stirrup. "We're burnin' time standing here jawin'. Let's get to it."

"Not we, Ben—me."

"Look here, if you think—"

"Maybe you didn't hear what I just said to Carlos about responsibility. Burnt Rock is yours. You've got drunken gunfighters walking your streets. You've got more trouble than ten men could handle. What you don't have is the time to leave your town to go on a ride with me."

Ben chewed his lower lip for a moment. When he nodded, his head barely moved. He knew Monte was right. But that didn't make it any easier to swallow.

"No way around it," Monte said quietly.

113

Ben nodded. "They've got more'n half a day lead already," he noted. "Chances are they'll keep riding, at least till the deadline I gave them is over. One thing those herders know is how to put miles on a horse without wrecking him. They can cover a lot of ground."

"That's the way I'd do it," Monte said. "Keep moving. I don't think they'd be stupid enough to kill Bessie yet. They need her. What they're doing short of killing her I don't know and can't afford to think about. Because if I do, I'd set up outside of that Long Snake camp and drop those scum one at a time until the barrel of my Sharps melts off. Then I'd have my Colts and my knives—and my fists and my boots, for that matter." Monte looked at the river for a full minute. Ben said nothing.

"But I'm not going to do any of that, Ben. I'm going to follow the river and watch for tracks, like I said. But I need you to do something for me."

"Sure. What's that?"

"I still want to talk to the town. See that the notices get printed up, and pay some kids to tack them up all over town. I'll be back midday Sunday and come right to the church."

Ben nodded. "Anythin' else?"

"Yes. A prayer wouldn't hurt." Monte clucked his horse ahead and headed down the middle of the shallow river.

It took a moment for his comment to register in Ben's mind. *A prayer?* he thought. *Since when does Monte Krupp care about prayers?*

Bessie's face was a greasy, livid red from the unending hours in the saddle. Her work at the café afforded her little time in the sun, and she was without the deep tan that protected most West Texans. Blisters had formed and then were sandpapered away by the length of rough rope that held her hands tied in front of her. The flesh around her wrists was raw and suppurating, her naturally healing fluids weeping away. She swayed in the saddle like a drunken cowboy, dizzy, fevered, unable to focus her eyes. "Water," she gasped from a parched mouth and sun-swollen lips. "I need water."

The man on the Appaloosa ahead of her who was leading her horse turned in his saddle and grinned at her. "I need a barrel of cold beer, a beefsteak, an' a dance-hall girl, lady. You don't see me moanin' about it. Shaddup."

"Kid!" A raspy voice called from behind Bessie. "Let her git down an' drink fer a minnit. It ain't like there's no water around. She's about to fall outta her saddle."

The man on the Appaloosa drew rein. The line of riders—Bessie and four men, one in front of her and three behind—were about eight or ten feet out into the Dos Gatos River, where the water was knee-deep on the horses. The current was sluggish but was moving well enough to almost immediately sweep away sediment and sand disturbed by the animals' hooves.

The lead man turned in his saddle again and looked back past Bessie to the speaker. "You givin' me orders now, Lou?"

"Nah, Kid, I ain't givin' you orders. But why not let the girl wet her face an' git a drink? I tell ya, she's gonna croak from sunstroke on us if ya don't."

Bessie stared down at the sparkling clear water moving past her. There were ripples where the flow parted to pass a jagged rock. Her throat moved in involuntary swallowing motions.

"We ain't got time to stop," the man named Kid said and clucked to his horse.

Bessie threw herself to the left, toward the middle of the river. Her legs were cramped from the unaccustomed hours in the saddle, and at first they refused to supply the strength she needed to heft herself from the saddle. The weight of her upper body helped. She hit the water on her side like a sack of rocks, and floated just about as well. Her feet jerked clumsily against the silty river bottom, and the sharp, wrenching cold of the water worsened rather than eased the cramps in her legs. She gulped water, choking on it, ignoring the spasms and pain of her throat, until a spark of fear flickered in her mind.

She couldn't stand up—couldn't even get her knees under her to poke her head above the surface. She drew in what should have been air but was, in her panic, water. Her hands, locked together by the rope, pawed ineffectually at the water that she had wanted—needed—badly enough to risk being riddled by her captor's bullets. Black spots, like floating patches of the deepest night, appeared before her. Her struggles lessened, and the pain was almost gone. Then she felt something snag her hair and pull hard against it.

And then the respite was over, and she was gasping, vomiting, and crying all at the same time. Her chest felt like she'd been struck by a battering ram. Kid, one hand locked in her hair and the other clutching his saddle horn against her weight, held her out of the water like a prize fish. Another rider appeared next to her, and the two men muscled her almost-limp body into her saddle.

She slumped forward, her head in her horse's mane. Water drained from her nose and mouth, mixed with bile and sand. She retched for what seemed like forever. A strong hand dragged her head up by her hair.

It was Kid. "You try anything smart again an' I'll kill you. You hear me?"

She had no voice.

"Answer me!"

"Yes," she gasped.

Monte Krupp fought against pushing the horse. He didn't know the animal well—this wasn't his own Daisy who could go forever—and he didn't know what sort of endurance the dusty, roan-colored gelding possessed. The going was achingly slow. The Dos Gatos was a quirky river that ran from what looked like a shallow stream in places to an almost pondlike expanse with thick stands of cattails and marsh grass on both shores.

Monte knew the kidnappers were keeping their horses in the water, but it was necessary for him to check the shores on both sides with a monotonous and time-eating frequency to make sure the gang hadn't left the river to veer off on one side or the other.

Monte's eyes were constantly in motion, sweeping both shorelines, picking out any cover large enough to conceal a man with a rifle. Ambush was a very real possibility, and the sound of the river rushing on its way was more than adequate to mask the sound of a horseshoe clinking against a stone or a lever-action rifle being cocked.

The sun above him seemed to be stuck in the same position in the sky, but his mount was showing signs of fatigue, indicating that time was in fact passing. The Dos Gatos had gotten wider too, and more trips to the shorelines were required. A couple of times the gelding stepped off sandbars or shelves into ten or twelve feet of water, and this horse was one of those who didn't like to swim. The gelding squealed and churned his legs like a berserk stern-wheeler, expending more energy in a few moments than if he'd galloped a mile.

Late into the afternoon Monte reined in to a straggly copse of desert pine and scrub and unsaddled the horse, tying him securely but allowing him enough rope to graze. There were rabbit and bird tracks in abundance along the shore. Monte spread his saddle blanket to dry and walked a hundred yards down the river. When he found a good place to sit with his back against a wagon-wheel-sized boulder, he drew a Colt from his right holster with his left hand, clicked the cylinder so that a live round was chambered, and waited.

A scrawny range hen and five chicks edged out from the brush to the water, but Monte ignored them—too much trouble for too little meat. And the chicks still carried the fluff of the freshly hatched. If he killed the mother, he knew the babies would die as well.

A few moments later, Monte's supper sidled out from a tangle of brush and peered up and down the Dos Gatos, his oversized jackrabbit ears as alert as those of the finest quarter horse. The jack froze in place and then moved toward the water, moving carefully, suspiciously, like a front-line sentry. Monte began to swing the barrel of the Colt toward the rabbit and then stopped the motion. The outlaws were probably too far ahead to even hear a shotgun blast, much less a round from a .45. Even so . . .

His right hand eased down toward his boot and withdrew the knife hidden there in its sheath. After he flicked the weapon up, he caught the tip of its blade between his thumb and forefinger in what appeared to be a single, fluid motion. He flexed his wrist slowly one time to loosen the muscles, and then his hand darted forward, as if he were pitching a rock.

118

He carried the big jack back to where he'd left his horse, holding the rabbit by its rear feet to allow it to bleed out on the way. The meat was stringy, tough, and gamy tasting, but it was sustenance. The big chunks—the rear haunches in particular—almost cried out to be pierced by sticks and broiled over a fire so that the dripping, blazing fat would sweeten the meat. But a finger of smoke in the sky would point to him like a signal to the outlaws. Maybe they'd think it a drifter's fire or an Indian's camp—but maybe they wouldn't.

Monte paced as his horse grazed languidly. In the hour that they'd been stopped, the horse seemed to regain some of his stamina. Now that the gelding's hunger was sated, he pushed his muzzle into the grass almost perfunctorily, seeking out only the greenest clumps. The speckled shade afforded by the stand of trees was growing darker.

As Monte bent to pick up his blanket, the voice from behind startled him. He spun around, his right hand drawing a Colt.

"You'd be the fella they called 'the Deathling.'" The voice was low and flat and a bit raspy but carried no emotion. "Might jist as well holster that side arm."

The barrels of the man's shotgun stared impassively at Monte's chest, their gaping bores like a pair of tunnels to death. The man was tall and gaunt, but his bare arms were well-muscled. He wore a deerskin vest and a pair of leather pants, and moccasins rather than boots. With hair more gray than dark, a beard reached a foot down his chest.

Monte let the Colt slide back into his holster. "Something you want from me, mister?" he asked.

"I 'member you from years back," the man said. "The boys on both sides called you an' your pard the Deathlings. 'Cause you was so sudden, an' how a man'd be on his way to the afterlife 'fore he heard the shot from them big guns that took him down. Troops was scared of you two."

Monte held the man's eyes with his own. He saw no anger in them, no lunacy. In fact, he saw next to nothing there beyond, perhaps, a mild curiosity.

"Who are you?" Monte asked.

"Don't matter none, but my name's Brady. I seen you an' your pard at both battles at Manassas an' then again at the Peach Orchard. Fact is, I seen you settin' way up in a ol' sycamore tree outside the orchard, eatin' a fried chicken laig. You put the grub down on your ammo sack in the crotch of the tree way up there an' hefted yer Sharps and touched off a round that killed a major down the other side of the long trench—mebbe three, three-hundred-fifty yards. Then you picked up the chicken laig an' got to gnawin' it again, like you hadn't done nothin' but brush off a fly. Seein' you do that scared me. Scared me so bad I ran that night an' never went back." He stopped for a moment, trying to capture a thought, and then continued.

"I deserted, is what I done. I knew them other boys down the hill, they had their own sappers, jus' like you Deathlings. Seemed like I could feel the sights of a big gun levelin' in on me. So I run."

"That was war," Monte said. "And it was a long time ago."

"Not so long."

Monte let his hands fall to his sides. The silence between the two men was strangely—bizarrely—amicable, perhaps because of Brady's tone of voice. If it were not for the shotgun the deserter held, he could have been discussing last year's second cutting of hay.

120

"The other Deathling in the ground yet?" Brady asked. "See, I can't fathom how a man like you or him coulda kept on drawin' breath after Appomattox, seein' what you done."

"Like I said, it was a war. We got our orders, and we did what we needed to."

"The thing is, I let a fellow up at Second Manassas. I coulda skewered him like a autumn pig—had my bayonet already touchin' his throat, already drawin' blood. I couldn't kill him. I let him up, an' we both run off back to our lines." He paused again. "You an' the other Deathling never did nothin' like that, did you? You Deathlings always squeezed the trigger, ain't that—"

"Don't call us that again."

The man's shotgun had been perfectly level and as steady as a tombstone. When the barrels moved, Monte flinched instinctively, his hands darting to his pistols. Brady didn't react. Instead, he continued lowering the shotgun until its muzzle almost touched the ground.

"I jist don't see how you could do it. I've seen you eatin' that chicken laig ever' day since you killed that major."

Monte crouched again to pick up his saddle blanket. He could feel Brady's eyes on him as he walked to his horse.

For the first time, Brady's voice showed emotion. "How could you do what you done?" he asked, almost in a whisper.

Monte placed his blanket on the roan's withers, smoothed it out, and hefted his saddle into place. "I'm not sure," he said, not turning to face the man. "I'm not sure at all. Everything's different now, though. Everything's changed." He set the front cinch and buckled the rear.

"You're followin' them boys travelin' with the woman," Brady said, his voice returning to normal.

Monte turned around quickly. "You saw them? How long ago? How did the woman look?"

"I seen them come by earlier today. They was movin' good, ridin' good stock, 'cept for the lady. Her horse was draggin' his toes—right worn out. A couple of the fellas was drinkin' whiskey, but nobody seemed drunk."

"How about the lady? Was she all right?"

"Wouldn't be no lady if she was runnin' with scum like that. But she—"

"She was kidnapped by them," Monte snarled.

Looking offended, Brady took a step back before answering. "She didn't look real happy, but she was settin' up in her saddle okay, best I could see. I seen her face looked a tad burned by the sun, is all. Her hands was tied in front of her. Must be a city woman, huh?"

"You saw that, and you watched them ride on by?"

Brady looked away from Monte's eyes. "See, it weren't none of my business. There were four of 'em, an' they was armed good. I couldna done nothin' without gettin' killed. Weren't none of my affair. I don' bother people. They was the first humans I seen in almost two months. I keep away from others an' their troubles. Have since the war."

"You didn't think to maybe follow them? Maybe figure out how to get the woman free?"

Brady's voice took on a whining tone that tossed kerosene on the already flaming hearth of Monte Krupp's anger. "I got no horse," he said. "I been walkin' all these years, an' I'm gonna keep on walkin'."

Monte swung into his saddle. "You asked me how I could do what I did during the war. Now let me ask you a question: How can you still be the coward you were when you deserted your unit?"

The barrel of the shotgun shifted slightly. Brady's words trembled. "You can't talk to me like that, Mr. Deathling. I—"

"You attempt to raise that shotgun, and I'll drop you right here and leave you for the vultures." Monte opened his coat. "Try it, Brady."

A moment passed with Brady staring at the ground. Then he opened his hand, and his weapon dropped to the dirt at his side.

"I'll tell you something else," Monte said. "When I said everything changed in my life, I meant it. But that doesn't mean I cotton to having a weapon pointed at me by a coward. You got lucky today. Maybe you ought to thank God for that."

Monte rode in the Dos Gatos until almost dark before he noticed that the reins were clenched so tightly in his left hand that his knuckles were white. He reined in and breathed deeply, doing his best to allow the blood-lust that had almost taken over him escape into the night air.

He was still relatively new at praying. It took him several tries and a good piece of time before he could communicate with the Lord. But when he did, his mind cleared, and he saw what he was doing as clearly as if a dense fog had been swept away by a sharp breeze.

There was no way he was going to catch up with Bessie and her abductors. Just as Bessie's horse had no doubt failed by now, so soon would the roan. The outlaws would double Bessie up with them on their own horses for a couple of hours at a time and continue at their same speed. He would be left afoot.

When he swung back in the direction from which he'd come, it was one of the most difficult things he'd ever done in his life. But he had no choice. Those herds of almost countless longhorns menaced the people and town of Burnt Rock like an advancing cavalry from Hades, and he needed to do his best to prevent the carnage he knew could occur.

None of that made the long ride back to Burnt Rock any easier for him, though.

7

Lee stood at the head of the gaping hole that contained the pine box, her Bible open in her hands. It didn't seem right that a man would be buried on such a magnificent day, a day alive with the sounds of nature, the smells of wild grass and the sweetness of the meandering breeze, and the morning warmth of the sun.

Carlos stood on Lee's right, a step or so back, Maria next to him, a handkerchief to her face. The men of the Busted Thumb shuffled their boots in the dirt, eyes downcast, hats clutched in their hands. They'd shaved, combed their hair, and wore their best Sunday-meeting clothing out of respect for Sy Younghans.

Lee struggled a bit with her voice as she read. Sy had been with the ranch since Lee first came to Burnt Rock. A quiet man who spent his off-duty hours with the Bible and the plays of William Shakespeare, he was friendly with his peers but kept to himself. He was intuitive with horses: He knew what frightened or angered them, and he knew how to bring peace to them through his voice and the touch of his hands.

She closed her Bible, stood quietly for a moment, and then nodded to the two men who stood back a few feet from the grave with shovels in hand, next to mounds of fresh soil. The first dirt to hit the top of the pine coffin made a hollow, lonely sound. The group turned away before the coffin was completely covered.

"So be it," Lee said, climbing up onto the board seat of the wagon.

Carlos helped Maria up, then got on from the other side and took the reins. "Tomorrow, Monte talks to the town at church," he said. "The man, he ees a wreck. An' Mike O'Keefe, I never see nobody with eyes as . . . how do you say . . . flat. Without life."

"I'm going to town today to visit with Mike," Lee said. "How he'll receive me, I don't really know, since I was the one who sent Bessie off to—"

"No!" Maria said. "You don' say those things, Lee! You did nothing wrong. Mike, he weel hold his arms out to you as a friend an' as his daughter's friend." She put her arm over Lee's shoulder and hugged her. "Las' night I din't sleep good, an' I went outside to pray. I hear you cry. Sometimes, to cry ees good, no? But to blame your-self for something where there ees no blame ees no good."

Lee's voice stuck in her throat. She shook her head and rasped, "I should have insisted she stay the night. If I'd . . . if . . ."

"*If* ees a beeg word," Carlos said. "If the dog no stop to sniff the tree, he would have catch the rabbit, no? *If* ees silly, Lee. You done nothin' wrong."

Lee wiped her eyes with the back of her hand and forced a small smile. "I hope not. Anyway, I want to see Ben too. He's under a lot of pressure with the cattlemen, and now with Bessie missing and Sy murdered, I doubt that he's sleeping more than a few hours a night, and probably not eating much, either."

Carlos stopped the farm wagon behind Lee's house. "You will come back before dark, no?"

"Yes. I will." She hugged Maria and climbed down from the wagon. "We'll pray for Bessie and Ben and the town later tonight, then? After supper?"

"Sí. I tol' the men. Maybe you can bring Ben?"

"I'll ask him. But his hands are full. I'd be surprised if he can break away from town."

Lee watched as Carlos drove off toward the main barn. When she entered her home, it seemed strangely empty, as if something important had been removed from it. She stood at the sink and pump in the kitchen and gazed at the chair where Bessie had sat. Images of the young woman—the joy in her eyes, the love in her voice, the sheer fun she was having sharing her big secret—circled through her mind. When she turned away to go to her bedroom, she once again had to wipe the tears from her eyes.

Slick was subdued as Lee rode to Burnt Rock. Some horses, she believed, reacted to their owner's moods. She believed with her entire being that horses could and did experience love—and believed that since empathy was such an essential part of love, God had granted a degree of it to the best of his animal kingdom. A smile crossed her face when she recalled a conversation with Ben about the topic.

127

"Seems to me horses are often about as bright as turnips, Lee. We've both seen 1,200-pound stallions spook an' run from a dead prairie dog or a piece of tumbleweed blowin' by. That doesn't show a whole lot of intelligence."

"What about Snorty, Ben?"

"Well . . . 'course, Snorty, he's different."

"Does he love you?"

"Well, yeah."

"Do you love him?"

"Ummm . . . hang it, Lee, 'course I do. But like I said, he's different from other horses. Look, I got reports to fill out an' other chores to do . . ."

The rifle in Lee's saddle scabbard banged her knee as she put Slick into a gallop. The stallion's raw power and phenomenal speed washed away Lee's sense of loss for her friend Sy and her trepidation over Bessie, at least for a few exhilarating moments. Then, like the constant beat of a muted drum, the weight of her pain broke through the momentary release.

She reined Slick to the far side of the street as she entered town, keeping as far from the Drovers' Inn as she could. The five or six horses in front of the saloon stood in mud but snuffed at an empty trough; someone had shotgunned the trough when it was full, and the water was seeping into the dirt of Main Street. In the alley next to the Inn a man slept on his back, snoring raucously, an empty whiskey bottle clutched to his chest with both hands.

Three men pushed through the batwings and stood gaping in the bright sunlight. That they were from the herds was obvious—they were drunk, dirty, loud, and profane. Some shouts and braying laughter were directed at her, she knew, but she clucked to Slick to pick up his pace as her only response. Still, she'd heard their words, and her face blushed and a bead of sweat broke from under her Stetson and trickled down her forehead.

O'Keefe's Café was locked and dark. Lee tied Slick at the hitching rail in front of the restaurant and walked into the alley next to the building. As she went up the outside stairs to the second floor, the dry wood creaked and groaned under her boots. Mike had tacked to the door a piece of butcher paper with a few words written in pencil.

Cafe is clossed till Bessie is back.
Plese pray for Bessie. Dont nock
Im not having company
—Michael O'Keefe.

Lee knocked lightly on the door. There was no response. She knocked louder, more insistently. When there was no answer, she twisted the doorknob and pushed the door inward.

Mike O'Keefe sat at a table in the semidarkness. His big hands were resting in front of him, and his eyes, red-rimmed from sleeplessness and tears, stared down at his motionless hands. A thick wave of the fetid, sickeningly sweet odor of rotting food hit Lee as she stood in the doorway. Her eyes quickly found the source: A roast, two casserole dishes, a pitcher of buttermilk, a platter of fried chicken, and a crock of soup rested on the counter near the potbellied stove, obviously untouched since caring friends had dropped them off for Mike.

"It's Lee," she said, moving toward the man.

Mike's eyes moved up from the table slowly. He looked as if he hadn't shaved in days, and there were cavernous,

129

dark hollows under his eyes. Lee looked to his greasy and uncombed hair, then to the small, amber-colored bottle near his hands.

She put her hand over his. "Mike? She'll be back. Monte will get her back."

His voice sounded as if it came from inside a cave. "I can't cry no more. Isn't that awful? I can't cry no more for my little girl. I don't have no tears left."

Lee swallowed her own tears. "Mike, you need to eat and you need to sleep. Come back to the Thumb with me. Stay in my house or with Carlos and Maria until Bessie is back. You can't keep living like this."

It was as if Mike had gone deaf. He picked up the amber bottle. "Doc give this to me. He tol' me it would make me sleep. It don't, though. It jist makes me . . . I dunno. Hollow-like."

Lee stood back from the table. "I'll rent a surrey and be right back. We can pack up some of your things and get you to where you should be—with friends who care about you. I'll be back in a few minutes and we'll—"

The thud of boots on the stairs interrupted her. "Morning, Lee," Doc's voice said from behind her. He moved across the room and set his black bag on the table. Mike was staring at his hands again. Doc reached down and placed his index finger on Mike's pulse point, held it there for a moment, and then removed it. He stood looking down at his friend appraisingly. "Well," he said, "this has gone too far."

Lee turned to him, her eyes questioning. Doc pulled her over to the other side of the room.

"It's a shock, Lee. I thought *that*—" he nodded to the bottle on the table, "might help. I can see it didn't. Instead of easing off the pressure on him, it's had what's called a paradoxical reaction. I heard what you were

130

saying as I came up. Ordinarily, I'd say it's a fine idea. Thing is, I want him here until . . . until something happens."

"But Doc—this rotting food, the way Mike's acting. He can't be alone."

"I know. I talked to Missy Joplin and Sarry Hughes yesterday evening. They're going to take shifts with Mike—clean up this place, cook for him, make sure he eats. Missy is talking to other ladies from the church to alternate with her and Sarry. He won't be alone for a minute."

"Is there anything I can do?" Lee asked.

"Not right now," Doc answered. "I want to work with him a bit. Why don't you go on about your business, and I'll make sure you know what's happening. Maybe in a few days I'll ask you to take him in at your ranch. Okay?"

Lee couldn't keep the anguish from her voice. "I want to do something for Mike and Bessie! I feel so useless."

Doc shook his head slightly. "You know something? I feel useless too. I can go great guns on broken bones or croup or headaches or birthing babies, but I can't do a thing for a mind or a heart."

Lee could see the pain in his eyes. "All right," she whispered. "I'll go to Ben's office. Either I'll be here every day or I'll have someone else come to you for a report. All you need to do is say the word and I'll—"

"I know, Lee," Doc said, easing her toward the door. "I know. Now, let me do what I can."

Lee left the café and walked down the block to the marshall's office. Ben was at the stove pouring coffee as she walked in. Monte sat in the chair in front of Ben's desk. "I need some of that," Lee said as she dropped to a chair. "As hideous as your coffee is, it's better than no coffee at all."

131

"Good to see you, Lee," Monte said, his voice sounding forced.

Lee nodded. "And you, Monte. No news?"

He shook his head. "Where's Carlos?"

"Carlos? He's at the ranch. Why do you ask?"

Monte straightened in his chair. "Why do I ask? You shouldn't be riding alone is why I ask! We can't find one lost woman, much less two of them!"

"Monte!" Ben barked from across the room. "Enough! Lee's not our enemy here—and I don't want you talkin' to her like she is!"

Lee's nerves were already vibrating like a hard-picked string on a guitar. A hornet's nest of words invaded her mind—but didn't make it to her mouth. Monte was standing now, and before she could articulate her anger, his image registered in her heart. The always clean, always well-dressed Monte Krupp looked like a cowhand who hadn't seen a tub, razor, decent meal, or night's sleep in weeks. Large patches of sweat formed ragged circles under his arms, and his once-white shirt was gray with range dust and dirt.

"Wait," she said quietly. "Ben—Monte—just wait. We can't do this. We can't attack one another like timber wolves, no matter how upset we are about Bessie."

Ben clenched his fists. "I won't have him sayin'—"

"Ben . . ." Lee said, again quietly, with a plea in her voice. "Gentlemen, there are things that need to be said right here and right now. Please listen for just a moment and then join in with me." She closed her eyes for a few seconds before speaking.

"Our Father, who art in heaven, hallowed be thy name . . ." she recited quietly. Both Ben and Monte expelled breaths at the same time and joined in, their voices hesitant at first but then gaining strength. ". . . Lead us not into temptation but deliver us from evil. Amen."

A long moment passed, but there was no heat in the time, no animosity. The frustration and fear that had goaded the two men into snarling at one another were washed from the air by the holy words.

Lee turned to Ben. "How about that cup of sludge I asked for?"

Monte grunted and sat back down. "I'll have another mug too, just to get rid of it before it eats through the pot."

Lee dragged a chair away from the wall and pushed it into place next to Monte. "What's this?" she asked, smoothing the drawing in front of her on the desk.

"I guess you've heard about how I think we need to protect Burnt Rock from the longhorns. This is what I'm going to propose to the town tomorrow at church," he said. "Here's the town—Scott's Mercantile at the end of the block, the hotel at the other end. This line here," he said, pointing, "is the ditch I want. It'll be about fifty yards out from the buildings, loop around the church, and make sort of a big, sloppy rectangle. We'll fill it with hay, straw, paper—anything that'll burn. Then we'll saturate it with kerosene and oil as thoroughly as we can."

"Looks like a lot of work and time," Lee said dubiously.

"It is," Ben said. "But Monte's been tellin' me some stories about what he's seen of stampedes, and I'm behind him 100 percent on this. The thing is, we'll need everyone who can swing a pick or handle a shovel to be involved."

"I'll donate all the straw and hay I can," Lee said. "And we have a few barrels of kerosene out at the Thumb too."

"Maybe a few of your men can help with the diggin'," Ben suggested. "In short shifts, so that the ranch work gets done too."

Lee studied the drawing for a few moments. "If this really happens, what about the people out on the farms between the herds and the town?"

"Good point," Monte said. "But I think it's covered. I'm going to ask that the church bell not be used at all until this thing is over, and that we keep someone at the bell twenty-four hours a day, seven days a week. The tolling of the bell carries at least to the farms when it's rung hard. As soon as anyone hears it, they should drop whatever they're doing and head for town at a dead run."

Lee nodded. "I see. We'll need to make arrangements so that all the old folks or anyone who's sick or bedridden can be brought in too. How about if I check around on that so no one gets left behind?"

"Good, Lee. You do that," Monte said.

"One other thing," Ben added. "Day after tomorrow's the fifth day—the end of the time I gave Toole and the rest of them. I'm goin' out to the Long Snake Camp then. You ridin' with me, Monte? I'm not lookin' to go to war, but I got some things that need to be said."

Monte's eyes met Ben's, and they burned with an icy fire. "Yeah—I'll be with you. I've got some things to say too."

The church was overflowing with people. The pews were full, and the children had been sent outside to play after the worship to make room for adults. The aisles were jammed with standing men and women, and the balance of those attending stood outside the broad front doors.

Monte Krupp, bathed and shaved, strode to the front and stood behind the lectern. The buzzing of conversation stopped, and after a moment, the church was as quiet as a forgotten tomb. Monte knew he looked haggard. He'd had no choice but to look at himself in a mirror that morning while he was shaving. His eyes had seemed to be set in deep hollows, and there was pain in them that he was sure not one of the congregation could miss. When he spoke his voice was deep and resonant and carried to those outside the building.

"I'm glad the youngsters are outside," he began. "Some of what I'm going to say here isn't pretty. No— that's wrong. *None* of what I'm going to say here is pretty. If I didn't believe this was a matter of life and death, I wouldn't be here. I'll ask you to hear me out, and then I'll answer any questions anyone has."

He paused a moment. "Just before the war I was following a herd of maybe a thousand head of buffalo outside a little town in Oklahoma called Hull's Creek. It was a bit smaller than Burnt Rock, but not by much. I say 'was,' because the town isn't there any longer. What is there is a scattered pile of ripped apart wood and bits of glass and torn up rags and the bones of horses and dogs and men and women—and children. There are plenty of human remains still there, buried under what used to be the town. A fire that probably started at the blacksmith's shop after the buildings were leveled made rescue impossible. The whole town of Hull's Creek died that day. I survived because I was on a steep little wooded rise, and I was close enough to see the entire ungodly spectacle." Monte stood motionless and silent for a moment.

"It wasn't the fire that murdered the town. It was a thousand head of buffalo in a stampede. They swept through that little burg like a wave of pure, destructive evil, ladies and gentlemen. I've seen tornado wreckage and I've seen what a hurricane can do—and I've lived through the worst and bloodiest battles of the War Between the States. Nowhere—nowhere have I seen carnage like I saw that day. I watched a big barn move—the whole huge structure moved fifty feet when the main part of the herd hit—skidding along, boards and beams flying off of it, the wood screaming as it was twisted and broken—and then the whole building simply went down and those buffalo ran over it. The broken boards acted like spears when the thousand-pound bulls hit them, and there was blood spraying in the air and writhing animals harpooned like whales, and that didn't even slow the stampede. They hit the house next, and it went down as if it'd been built of playing cards. A family of a farmer, his wife, and six kids lived there. None of them made it."

As he walked a couple of steps away from the lectern, Monte allowed what he'd said to settle in the minds of the gathering. Husbands and wives, he noticed, were clutching one another. There wasn't a sound—not the creaking of a pew or a cough—when he went on.

"Most stampedes take place at night, but the one in Hull's Creek was during the day. What set the herd running was a little hailstorm that didn't last two minutes. Hail is real rare around there. It panicked some of the buffalo, and they ran. But you need to understand that there's no logic or reason behind a stampede. I've seen much smaller ones start when a couple of bulls are fighting. They scare some cows with calves at their sides, and those run and the rest follow. I heard that a fellow on a cattle drive down toward Abilene started playing an accordion—one of those squeeze boxes—and that set off the herd. Lots of folks think thunder will start a run, but that's not really true. As dumb as those creatures are, they've heard plenty of thunder throughout their lives. They don't much like it, and they might get nervous or feisty, but that's all. Lightning, now, that's a different thing. If one in the herd is struck, particularly near the center of a bunch, they're going to panic and run."

Monte walked back to the lectern and placed his hands on it. "There are no guarantees about what'll start a panic. Like I said, lightning is bad. There's one kind of lightning that scares the animals and the cowboys about equally, but it's very rare. It's called St. Elmo's fire—but I doubt that we need to worry about it. I don't know that I've ever heard about it occurring this far west."

"What is this St. Elmer's fire thing?" a voice called from the back.

"St. Elmo's—not Elmer's. I don't know what causes it, but it can follow ball lightning—lightning that sort of collects into a burning ball and rolls around on land or water. The St. Elmo's part is . . . well . . . lumps of a strange, hissing blue light that touch on things and then leap to others. I hear it happens at sea a lot—whips around on the masts, setting fire to whatever it touches."

There was silence in the church until Monte continued.

"I can tell you folks this: If those herds outside of town stampede, they'll destroy Burnt Rock and everything and everyone in it. They'll make Sherman's march through Atlanta look like a grade-school picnic."

Monte paused for a moment. "There's nothing I know of that can stop a stampede once it's going full-tilt, but there's something that can turn one: fire. I've seen it work. Now, here's what I propose we do . . ."

Ben started passing Monte's rough drawing around as Monte explained his plan. It took less than a couple of minutes. Before he was completely finished speaking, a voice from the group outside the church bellowed, "Let's quit wastin' time an' git to diggin'!"

Missy Joplin, the oldest and no doubt feistiest resident of Burnt Rock, was one of the first to pull her two-seat surrey up to the rear of Scott's Mercantile. Next to her rode a pair of chocolate-frosted cakes on a wooden tray.

Lee led Muffin, Missy's old mare, to a hitching rail. "I don't know how you do it, Missy," she laughed. "The meeting hasn't been over an hour, and you're here with food for the workers."

"'Course I am. I don't see no one else offerin' to feed our menfolk while they dig this moat. You modern women is all off runnin' ranches an' such."

Lee laughed again. "Right, Missy. Next we're going to want to vote and run for president too!"

"You hush, Lee Morgan," Missy warned. "I've still got a willow switch in my closet that got my own boys a-yelpin' when they smart-mouthed me. I don't doubt it'd work on you!" Missy climbed down from her surrey, ignoring Lee's hand to assist her. "Thing is, I had just started them cakes afore I left for church. I was gonna take one to Mike O'Keefe an' the other to Ben."

Ben rode up on Snorty and tied him near Missy's surrey. He reached out an index finger toward the nearest cake.

"Hold it right there, Ben!" Missy bellowed. "You leave that frostin' an' them cakes alone till you've done some work!"

Other men and even entire families were arriving, some on wagons or farm carts, some on horseback, and some on foot. Most carried picks or shovels. Mr. Scott wheeled a garden seed-spreader from the loading dock of his store while carrying a fifty-pound sack of quick-lime over his shoulder. Lee, Missy, and Ben gawked at the middle-aged merchant as if he were an apparition.

"Well," Mr. Scott said, "what's the problem? Have you folks never seen a man ready to go to work before?"

"Umm . . . Mr. Scott . . ." Ben said. "It's just that we've never seen you out of your suit an' tie an' shined-up shoes. Kind of set me back a stride, ya know?"

"Stride or not," Scott harrumphed, "let's get to it. This little seeder will put down a nice white line to show these boys where to dig. Without a reference, we'll have trenches going all over the place." He looked at Ben. "About fifty yards out from the buildings?" he asked. "That's what Monte said, wasn't it?"

"Yessir. It was. You might want to tell them we're not diggin' wells here—an honest four feet will be deep enough. Since you seem to be doin' the thinkin' here, Mr. Scott, how about you headin' up the operation?"

Scott pinned the marshall with his eyes. "Now, what does it look like I'm already doing, Ben?" The merchant muttered a couple of other words that couldn't be heard and began dumping the quicklime into the seeder's hopper. "You—Jimmy Frankenberger!" Scott shouted in a tone of voice and with volume that was completely out of character with his mild, almost obsequious, storekeeper persona. "Heft up this sack of lime and follow me to fill the hopper when I run out. You others quit leaning on your shovels and get to work. This ain't a party, boys. We got digging to do!"

Ben and Lee faced one another, incredulous. *"Ain't?"* Lee whispered. "Mr. Scott has never said that word before in his life."

"Probably not," Ben agreed, laughing. "But I think he'll have a lot more to say before this project's done. Lookit the way Doc handles a shovel—like he's never seen one before. And ol' Mr. Maxwell's gonna take somebody's head off, the way he's swingin' that pickax. These fellas are storekeepers and professional men, not laborers."

139

"Wait till the farmers get here, Ben. Between them and Mr. Scott, this fire line will be finished before supper."

The clang of shovels against rocks filled the air. "Don't bet on it, Lee. Hear all that? This ground is so filled with rocks, it's like tryin' to dig through steel. And rain has been so scarce, the soil's set up like stone." He shook his head. "Gonna take some time."

"How long do you think?"

"I can't say. That depends on how much time we can all give to the work. It could be a week, maybe a few days over a week."

Lee watched the men at work for a minute. "I'll head back to the Thumb and have our biggest wagon loaded up with straw, and see if some of the men care to make some extra wages."

"You shouldn't have to pay money out of your own pocket, Lee. You're donatin' the hay and straw, and that's—"

Lee shook her head. "It's Sunday, and I don't ask my hands to work on their day off unless it's a real emergency. Those men give me an honest day's work every day, and I'm grateful. They deserve to be compensated for what they do here today. During the week, after their day is over at the ranch, they can volunteer as they see fit—and I'm sure lots of them will. But today . . ."

Ben's respect was clear in his voice. "Did you ever consider that it's just that attitude that makes the crew at the Busted Thumb so loyal to you?"

She considered for a moment. "No," she said with a grin. "It's Maria's cooking."

Lee tightened Slick's cinch and mounted. It was a glorious morning, and the still air was pure and not yet midday hot. Slick covered ground at a fast lope, his muscles working under her as steadily as the mechanism of a fine watch. Her eyes scanned the prairie around her, and off to the west she noticed some dust in the air—a rider, perhaps two, was heading toward Burnt Rock.

She reached down with her hand to touch the stock of the rifle in the scabbard at her right knee. The wood was smooth and warm from the sun and pleasant to touch. Still, the fact that she'd automatically checked on her weapon bothered her. Why should a plume of grit put into the air by a farmer going visiting or someone riding to town for a Sunday meal at the hotel make her think of danger?

Things hadn't been that way before the bridge went out and the herds came.

8

A couple of riders heading toward town isn't strange, Lee thought. *But a couple more coming from the opposite direction, putting me and Slick at the point of a triangle, could mean trouble.*

Or it could mean nothing at all.

Lee watched the new plume of dust moving toward her and then shifted her head to see that the original dust trail in the sky was closing in. She couldn't quite hear the horses yet, but Slick could, and his ears flicked back and forth and his nostrils spread as he tried to pick a scent out of the still prairie air.

The gritty fingers pointing at her position drew nearer, and the bass note of thudding hooves reached her. Slick sidestepped and snorted. Lee wiped the dampness from the palm of her right hand on her long Sunday skirt and drew the 30.06 from the scabbard at her knee. She was a dozen or so miles from the Busted Thumb and perhaps eight or ten miles from Burnt Rock. There wasn't a horse in West Texas that could catch Slick in either direction, she believed. But if this was some sort of trapping move, even her prize stallion couldn't outrun a bullet.

She chided herself for being a frightened child, but just in case, she jacked a round into the chamber of her weapon and clucked to her mount, holding to a fast lope. The paths of the two extended smudges in the sky shifted slightly but perceptibly toward her. Still, she held the lope. If she needed to run, she wanted Slick to have enough bottom left to keep as much distance as possible between herself and danger.

She pointed her horse to the center of a long rise, with her rifle clutched in her right hand and the reins held in her left. She felt Slick's muscles tighten a bit as he began up the grade. It was then that the two sets of riders came into view—two men on her left and two on her right. Even at that distance she could see that they were cattlemen by the way they moved with their horses, the casual ease born of years in the saddle. And they were riding at speed.

After Lee applied leg pressure, Slick increased his gait, now reaching far ahead of himself and pulling the hill at a gallop. She didn't have to check on her pursuers— she could hear them clearly now, the pounding of hooves, the creak of a saddle.

Slick shot over the top of the rise and snorted again, as startled as his rider. Three men sat twenty or so yards apart on their horses in a line just over the top of the hill. One was smoking, his leg cocked in front of his saddle horn, bluish cigarette smoke drifting languidly upward. Lee raised her rifle to her shoulder a heartbeat after the three men had done the same, the muzzles of their rifles pointing at her.

The other riders topped the hill to her sides and effectively boxed her in the space between the two groups. She veered Slick into a grinding left turn, but a cowboy with a loop whirling over his head was streaking toward her at a gallop. She wrenched Slick to her right, and two riders, turning hard, plugged the bit of open running space as effectively as a wooden bung does a barrel of water.

Her mind churned with fear—these had to be the men who'd taken Bessie and killed Sy. A prayer formed in her mind—and at the same time an idea flashed into life and began to grow. She spun Slick, seeking a way out of the trap. The two men to her right were the farthest apart—if she could slide between them and get to the open ground . . .

She felt a sharp, lashlike pain on her left shoulder, and then she was in the air, her arms pinned to her sides by the stinging bite of the rough rope that had encircled her. Her rifle spun away as she slammed into the ground on her back and shoulders. Her breath left her in a *woof*, and the back of her head hammered the ground once and then again as she was dragged by the roper. At the first impact, motes of black and red floated lazily across her vision. At the second, the darker motes took over, circling around and chasing off the red ones until all that was left was a thick darkness.

". . . ain't dead. All she took was a lil' thump on the head. See? She's breathin' good. Here, gimme yer canteen."

The voice, raspy from smoke and whiskey, seemed to be coming from far away—maybe from inside a tunnel or a well. Lee heard the words but didn't quite understand them. Who was he talking about? Bessie? Whose voice was it? What happened?

Tepid water sloshed over her face and into her open, dirt-encrusted mouth. Her chest was wracked by a powerful cough, and she felt as if she'd swallowed a blacksmith's fire. Sitting up, she shook her head, gulping air and hacking at the same time. She tried to raise a hand to her face, but her arms were welded to her sides.

"Give 'er some slack—git yer rope offa her. She ain't goin' nowhere."

It was the voice again. Lee's arms were suddenly free. She scrubbed at her eyes with her hands, still gasping. Her eyes were raw from the grit, but her vision, filmy through tears, returned. The first thing she saw was a forest of horses' legs.

"You 'bout ready to ride, missy?" the voice asked.

Lee worked saliva into her mouth and cleaned some of the dirt from her lips and front teeth with the back of her hand. She looked up past a gray horse's chest, neck, and head to where a heavily bearded man sat looking down at her. As dazed as she was, the man's empty left eye socket and drooping lid that didn't quite close made her shudder with revulsion. She drew a deep breath and held it for a moment. Already, her mind was working. *No broken ribs—good.*

"We got some ground to cover. Stand up, missy."

The ground beneath Lee seemed to be moving. She shook her head, swallowed hard, struggled to her feet. The black motes threatened for a few long seconds and then receded.

"Who are you? What do you want?"

The one-eyed man grinned at her, showing discolored, randomly slanting teeth. "My friends, they call me One-Eye. We're jist takin' you on a lil' social call, is all. Seems like your marshall is all wrought up 'bout

146

your pal Bessie visitin' with us, so we thought we'd fetch her some comp'ny."

One of the riders guffawed. "Could be you an' her an' the rest of us, we'll have a little party? You like parties, doncha, honey? Have a lil' snort a' red-eye, maybe dance some with the boys?"

Anger was beginning to wash away shock from Lee's mind. The plan that had sparked a few moments ago flared brighter. These men would take her to Bessie. Together, she and her friend could work out an escape. She watched One-Eye. "You have Bessie?"

"Sure do," he said. "Problem is, she tore some skin offa my friend Malcolm's face when he was makin' friends with her. Ol' Mal, that boy has a temper on him like a hornet in a burnin' barn. He slapped her round a bit, tryin' to teach her some manners. Then, 'course, she tried to run off. Atticus, he seen to her with a whip for that."

"Where is she?"

"Ain't none of your nevermind till we get there. You mount up now, or we'll tie you over the saddle of that good horse of yours."

Slick stood to one side of the group of men. Lee took a tentative step toward him. The pain down her back and into her legs was prodding her now, and she knew it would get worse before it got better. Her hand started to her lower back, where it felt like a rock had ground into her flesh, but she stopped the motion and used the hand to wipe her face again. A long hobble—a thick leather belt with a buckle at each end—ran from her horse's right front leg to his left rear. It wouldn't impede him or give him too much trouble at slow gaits, but it'd be impossible for him to gallop or even lope without going down in a tangle of legs, rider, and hobbles.

"You jus' stay here on my right side an' you won't get hurt none," One-Eye said. "Atticus, he said not to kill you, but he tol' us if you git smart, we can deal with you how we see fit." He grinned. "I don't think you'd like that at all."

Lee began to mount. She winced, cried out in pain, and dropped back to the ground next to Slick, wobbling on her feet. Several of the men laughed. She raised her left foot again to the stirrup, grabbed the horn with both hands, and hauled herself up into her saddle.

"Little sore, are ya?" One-Eye asked.

"Not as sore as you're going to be when Ben Flood and Monte Krupp catch up with you outlaws," Lee said, proud that her voice conveyed disdain and anger—and not fear or pain.

"Monte? He's the cute lil' grasshopper with the Sharps, ain't he? Didn't he set out to run us down an' then turn yellow an' head back?" One-Eye spat to the side. "Ain't neither one of 'em two got the guts of a weasel, honey. Your marshall's keepin' right close to his town, an' his lil' friend seems to be spendin' his time preachin' at your church—I got boys keepin' an eye on the town." He looked over the riders around himself and Lee. "You boys kinda scared of the lawman an' the church boy?"

One-Eye's men apparently found him very funny—the sound of their laughter echoed off the prairie.

"You boys can bust out your bottles now an' have you a taste. We got our girl here, an' she ain't about to go nowhere 'cept where we're takin' her." One-Eye took a bottle offered to him, tugged the cork from its neck with his teeth, and spat it aside. He lifted the bottle and drank thirstily.

Lee couldn't move her gaze from the bobbing of the man's Adam's apple as he sucked down the whiskey. It surged up and dropped back like the head of a pecking rooster. The purplish-red scar tissue that circled his neck moved with the pulsing lump in his throat.

One-Eye lowered the bottle, belched, and caught Lee staring at him. "Gawkin' at my neck, are ya? Maybe you never seen a man who done the dance at the end of a rope an' lived to tell about it?" He belched again. "Lost my eye at the same time. See, 'fore I came on as one of Atticus's top hands, I done a bit of rustlin'. Some yahoos down toward the panhandle caught me with some of their beef. Was only a ricochet what took my eye out, but the eye's still gone jist as if it'd been a full slug. Then they strung me up." He drank from the bottle again and then tossed it to another rider. "Atticus and a few of his boys was comin' past an' seen what was happenin'. There I was, chokin' an' dancin', an' I alla sudden heard a gun fire, an' then I was on the ground, pullin' that noose offa my neck. The vittles I'd ate that mornin' jist spewed on outta my mouth like . . ."

Lee showed her abhorrence with a quick shake of her head and a grimace.

"The point is," One-Eye went on, "I figger I already been dead once, or close enough to it so it don't matter. That's why I ain't scared of them Deathlings or no other man. I'm kinda already in the ground."

"Deathlings?" Lee couldn't stop the word before she said it.

"Your friend the marshall never bothered to tell you that's what him an' his little pardner was called during the war? They was sappers, honey—they killed more men than any frontline boy on either side ever did." He smiled at the look on her face. "News to ya, huh?"

"The war was a long time ago," she said quietly.

"Hogwash, lil' lady," One-Eye laughed. "It ain't nearly over yet!"

They rode through the dusk toward the Dos Gatos, as Lee expected they would. Ben and Monte believed Bessie had been taken far down the river.

Slick, after a couple of miles, paid little attention to the hobbles. Lee held him at a steady, slow pace but allowed him to pick his way over and around rocks and prairie dog holes. One-Eye and Lee led the others into the river to fetlock depth, and they splashed along, covering miles fairly quickly but without rushing. Slick bared his teeth a few times at One-Eye's horse, but unless the other animal moved too close, he didn't pursue the fight. One-Eye reacted to the quibbling between the horses with hands as sure, practiced, and skilled as Lee's own. Whatever else the outlaw was, he was a horseman.

The sibilant splashing of the horses in the gently moving water accounted for the only sounds. Darkness had come, but the moon was generous this night, and the river glistened up ahead.

"Over here," One-Eye said, swinging his horse toward the far shore. Surprised, Lee followed, easing Slick in behind the man's horse. The water level rose to her boots, to her knees, and then began to drop again. The other men clustered behind her and One-Eye as they broke through scrub and weeds and into a stand of trees. One-Eye motioned a rider to take the lead, directly ahead of her. They followed the edge of what had once been a few acres of unharvested corn. The desiccated stalks rattled against one another as horses brushed past them.

A lopsided cabin stood beyond the cornfield in a splash of moonlight that showed the state of its disrepair but softened the sharp angles of the partially collapsed roof and the rough logs that jutted at an angle at one end of the structure. Lee smelled smoke from a cook fire—bacon was the strongest scent, but the bite of chicory coffee was there, as was the tang of spiced beans.

"Everything okay?" a voice called from the brush. "I see you got us another guest."

As they closed in on the ramshackle cabin, Lee saw a man step through the doorless opening. The cook fire was on the side of the cabin, and a pair of men leaned against the tipping wall of the building.

The man in the doorway walked the fifteen feet from the cabin to One-Eye's horse. "You done good," he said.

"I always do good, Atticus," Eye-One replied. "I tol' you I'd git her, an' I did."

Toole nodded. "Yeah," he said. He stepped closer to Slick. "Get down."

Lee exaggerated her stiffness and her pain—offering a short cry as she swung her right leg over the saddle. She stood next to her horse, reins in hand.

"You know who I am?" Toole asked.

"Probably Atticus Toole from the Long Snake herd," Lee said. "I've heard about you."

The angle of the moonlight gave Toole's eyes a chillingly catlike luster. His voice was deep, calm, but there was a threat behind it somehow, even in the few words he'd said. "You're gonna be here a while—you an' your friend inside. I heard you're fairly bright for a woman—own a big horse ranch an' all. Maybe that's good. Maybe you're smart enough not to make stupid mistakes. Your friend Bessie has already made a couple, an' she's paid for them too."

"If you've hurt Bessie—"

She didn't see Toole's hand move, but she felt the heat and power of his open palm against her face. She stumbled back against Slick and raised her hand to her cheek.

"That's what I mean about stupid things," Toole went on in the same tone of voice. "You don't do nothin' but listen when I talk. You keep your mouth shut 'less I ask you somethin'. You do what I tell you an' what the boys I leave here tell you."

Lee couldn't stop the tears running from her left eye, but she needed to show this man that she wasn't crying from pain or fear. She held Toole's eyes with her own, even though his face shimmered like a mirage through her tears.

Toole scratched the thick stubble on his chin without breaking his gaze. "Go on inside," he said. "Your friend's in there. Seems like she might need some tendin' to."

Lee held her glare for another second, biting back the words that filled her throat like molten steel. Then she spun and hurried toward the door.

It was as dark inside as out, but there was enough light to see what little the room contained. A homemade chair stood near the caved-in fireplace, and a three-legged table with one end propped up with a raw branch was centered in the room. Against the wall to the rear, Bessie was curled into a childlike position on what appeared to be three or four saddle blankets tossed over the wooden floor. The girl's face was turned from Lee, and the gold of her hair caught the light flooding in through the shards of glass that still remained in the frame of the small back window. Lee hurried to her friend's side and touched her shoulder gently.

Bessie was immediately awake and screaming. "No— no, please! No more!"

The same light that touched Bessie's hair so gently also revealed the livid puffiness under her right eye and the long slash that started at her left eyebrow and snaked down her face to her jaw.

"Oh, Bessie," Lee sobbed as she watched recognition replace the panic in the girl's eyes. "Oh, Bessie . . ."

The strength of Bessie's lunge into her arms made Lee's back and shoulders scream in pain as she grasped the younger woman. Bessie buried her face in Lee's shoulder and chest and sobbed as if the tears would wrench her body apart.

"I'm here, honey," Lee said, gently stroking Bessie's hair. "I'm here. We'll get out of this. I promise you, we'll get out of this."

"They . . . they horsewhipped me, Lee," Bessie sobbed. "I got out the back window the night they brought me here, an' I started runnin' in the woods. An' one of them almost trampled me on his horse, an' then he roped me like a calf and dragged me all the way back. An' then that boss man—Toole—he took a long whip, an' he hit me with it till I was jus' screamin' an' cryin' an' beggin' him to stop, but he wouldn't, an' he kept—"

"Hush, Bessie. Hush!" Lee insisted. "That's all over. We're together now." She touched her finger to Bessie's quivering lips but quickly withdrew it when she felt the swelling and scabs. "Hush," she repeated. "Nobody's going to hurt you anymore."

Bessie's trembling slowed as Lee held her. After a half hour had passed, the girl's breathing became soft and regular with sleep, and the death grip of her arm around Lee's neck relaxed.

Every hour or so, one of the thugs would lumber through the doorway, hold a lantern up high enough so that its harsh light illuminated the two women, and then go back outside.

Lee's sleep was shallow, and each time Bessie moaned, Lee woke up. The image of Toole and his horsewhip lashing out at her young friend brought the

153

bitter taste of bile to the back of her throat. When the young girl whimpered in her sleep, a hard nugget of wrath in Lee's heart began to glow with the fire of righteous anger.

She prayed as she waited for whatever the next day would bring, pleading for the Lord to give her the courage and cunning she knew she'd need to get Bessie and herself away. Her prayers calmed her, at least to a degree. But her mind wrestled with concepts that were new to her—new to her Christian spirit and new to the person she was.

Does Ben feel as I do when he faces men like this? Does he feel the . . . the hatred . . . I do at this moment? When his hand goes for his gun, does he believe that he's smashing his boot heel on a serpent? Can I actually do this? But if I don't—Lord Jesus, please help us . . .

Voices from the other side of the flimsy wall of the cabin brought Lee to consciousness. The cheerful light of the early morning seemed like a mockery.

". . . won't try a thing while we have the women. There's a buncha money in this thing for us—what we'll make for the stock we drift off from the herds an' sell ourselves when the train is runnin' again."

Lee recognized Atticus Toole as the speaker. It was One-Eye who responded. "That buffalo man has a big rep, though. An' Flood does too. I dunno, Atticus. You seen what that Krupp done with his big Sharps from a mile off. If he got in close and set up, he'd pick us off one by one till we was all dead."

Toole snorted. "That's my point. Long as we got them two women under lock an' key, ain't nobody gonna be shootin' at us. Look, there's only Flood to look after his town. Krupp's a wild card, but he figures we stayed in the river to the caves an' we're keeping his woman there.

154

He ain't gonna leave his Deathling partner alone, so they ain't gonna be doin' much searchin' for us. They can't. Long as our boys an' those from the other herds keep tearin' up the town—and they will, you can take that to the bank—the lawman an' Krupp will have plenty to keep them busy."

"What about after? When the cattle can be shipped? Then what do we do with the women?"

"We sell 'em to the Indians or the *vaqueros.*"

"Serve 'em right," One-Eye observed. "They's both uppity."

Lee smelled cigarette smoke and coffee in the air that drifted into the cabin. Bessie began to stir in her arms. When she moaned, Lee whispered into her ear. "Bessie, honey, you're going to have to be strong today. Don't make any noise. I want them to think we're still asleep. Okay?"

Bessie nodded.

"Do you know where the horses are? Are they tied or staked or closed in somehow?"

Bessie moved her mouth to Lee's ear. Even at a whisper her voice conveyed exhaustion and pain. "Kinda through the woods jus' behind here there's a little pond. They made me carry water for coffee, an' I saw it. They roped off a little corral there."

Lee thought for a moment. "Okay. Can you ride, Bessie? Would you be able to stay on a horse?"

"I . . . yeah. I will."

"Suppose we didn't have time for saddles, honey? What about then?"

"I haven't rode bareback but once or twice in my life, an' not since I was a little girl. Oh, Lee—if I fell off an' they got me again . . ."

"Hush. That's all right. We'll get you a saddle somehow."

Men moved around outside the cabin. One-Eye strode in through the door opening. "Git outside—the both of you. Rustle up some grub. Me an' the boys is hungry."

"Bessie's wounds need to be cleaned," Lee said. "That needs to be done first."

One-Eye stepped closer. Lee saw that he had a long blacksnake whip coiled over his shoulder. "You'd best start learnin' the rules right now, missy," he said. "Atticus is leavin' me in charge. That means I can use this here baby," he patted the whip, "when an' how I see fit. I'll let you wash her up a tad maybe later. Right now, git out here an' get some food goin'."

Lee and Bessie exited the cabin. Lee checked the fire, which was already burning well, and scraped the thick layer of coarse salt from a large lump of bacon and cut it into smaller pieces. Bessie, moving slowly, poured white beans into a kettle of water.

One-Eye stood close to Lee, watching her work. "Ain't gonna be much of a meal," he said. "I'll have one of the boys shoot somethin' for dinner."

Lee, ignoring the man, worked a sheath knife through the flint-hard bacon. Then she set the knife aside and put the cut meat into a skillet already resting on the edge of the fire. One-Eye watched the bacon sizzle for a few moments and then walked away from the fire toward the cabin. Lee shifted the skillet a bit, hovering over it. Her eyes hadn't left the knife since she'd dropped it a few moments ago.

Toole stood with his back to her, twenty feet or so away, drinking coffee. Two other men had gone to see to the horses. She quickly checked Bessie's position—she was stirring the kettle of beans.

Lee drew a deep breath, said a quick prayer, and eased back from the fire and the spitting bacon. Still crouched, she half turned and raised her left hand to her face, as if to push away strands of hair from her forehead. At the same time her right hand snaked out and clutched the knife. Suddenly, her back was on fire. The weighted end of the whip tore through the fabric of her dress and gouged a shallow laceration a foot long between her shoulders. She screamed and fell to the side, the excruciating pain radiating and sending spikes of agony down her back and into her arms.

"See what I mean?" One-Eye snarled. "You git cute, you're gonna git hurt." He coiled the lash and put it back over his shoulder.

Lee chewed back the pain and glared at the grinning man. Her hand begged to touch the wound, but she refused to give One-Eye the satisfaction of seeing her try to ease her pain.

A low moan escaped from Bessie, who stood with her hand to her mouth. Lee looked at her friend. Bessie's eyes told her more than her words could have—much more. It was as if Lee could hear the younger woman's thoughts. *Do something, Lee Morgan.*

Toole strode over. "Handy with that blacksnake, ain't he?" He tossed the grounds from his coffee mug into the fire and spoke to One-Eye. "I'm headin' back to the herd. I suspect Flood an' Krupp have already been lookin' for me there. Stan an' Will are stayin' here with you. I'll get some provisions out to you in the next couple of days." He took a cheroot from his vest pocket and scraped a match to light it. "I ain't gotta tell you how important them two women are," he said, exhaling smoke. "If they was to get away from you fellas, I'd be . . . well . . . unhappy."

One-Eye nodded. "Yessir."

"Fact is," Toole went on, "I'd kill all three of you boys without askin' no questions."

One-Eye swallowed and nodded again. "They ain't gonna git away," he said.

Toole took another drag on his cigar, exhaled a plume of smoke, and turned away, starting toward where the horses were kept.

"Git to that bacon 'fore it burns to cinders," One-Eye growled at Lee. "An' watch yer step."

Lee got her feet under her and tended to the bacon. She gritted her teeth against the streak of pain that burned across her back when she bent over. Looking up, she saw one of the men who'd gone to look after the horses riding in on a bay gelding. The man tied the animal to the collapsed porch railing and sauntered over to the fire. Shortly afterward the other rode up and tied his horse. Both were younger than One-Eye, and each carried a side arm in a tied-down holster.

Lee used a fork with a missing tine to spear chunks of bacon and drop them into the metal pans that were encrusted with the remains of previous meals. She walked around the fire, picked up the kettle of beans by its handle, and returned to where she'd set the plates. The eyes of the two men never left her. One-Eye, she saw, was sitting cross-legged a few feet away, rolling a cigarette. He too was armed with a holstered pistol.

If I'm going to do this, I've got to do it fast, she thought. She looked to the other side of the fire, caught Bessie's eyes, and mouthed *"Be ready."*

Lee started dumping beans from the kettle onto the individual plates lined on the ground in front of her, using a soiled cloth she found next to the fire to keep her hand from the hot surface of the kettle's edge. The metal handle was warm, but not enough to singe her skin, as the body of the kettle was.

She'd placed the plates a foot or so apart, the last one perhaps a yard from where the two men sat together.

She hesitated for a brief part of a moment and breathed a silent prayer.

She slopped a good helping of the steaming beans onto the first plate and did the same for the second. She shifted herself to stand over the third plate, tipped the kettle a bit, and then hurled the contents at the two wranglers. The beans left the kettle in a loose mass of hot, dripping pellets. She released the kettle, and it thunked off the chest of the near man, bringing a loud and frenzied howl of pain from him. The other pawed at his face and eyes, snarling like a tortured animal.

Lee dropped to her side, at the same time tearing the bottom of her blouse free from where it'd been tucked into her long Sunday skirt. The grips of the derringer she'd endured wearing for what seemed like forever slapped into her palm, and as she drew the pistol from its soft holster at the small of her back, her thumb found and cocked the hammers of both barrels.

One-Eye was halfway to his feet, his pistol just clearing leather and his mouth gaping open with surprise and anger. The barrel of his Colt pivoted upward.

Lee raised her arm and squeezed the first trigger. The derringer leaped in her hand and wrenched her wrist painfully with its kick. A black dot the size of a penny appeared in One-Eye's forehead, and he toppled backward.

Lee let her momentum carry her into a roll next to the fire, swinging her gunhand toward the two men. One was still clawing at his eyes and cursing. The other was leveling his pistol at her. She squeezed the second trigger, and again the derringer bucked in her hand. The cowboy went down, his arms splaying away from his body, his Colt turning over in an arc and then skidding into the brush. Lee was at One-Eye's corpse in a heartbeat, prying his pistol from his fingers.

The remaining cattleman, his face a mask of dripping beans, was reaching toward his side arm.

"Stop! Draw that and you're a dead man!" Lee shouted. He hesitated, his right hand hovering near the grips of his pistol. Lee clicked back the hammer of One-Eye's Colt. The metallic sound seemed as loud as the two rounds fired from the derringer. His hand stopped.

"Bessie!" Lee called. "Take his gun—now. Move!"

Bessie, both hands at her mouth, was like a statue.

"Now, Bessie!" Lee hollered. "Get that gun!"

The harsh command in Lee's voice galvanized Bessie into action. She hustled to the outlaw and dragged his pistol from his holster.

"Now cock it and hold it on him, Bessie—step back a bit and hold the gun on him. If he moves, pull the trigger."

Bessie gulped but obeyed, thumbing back the double-action hammer.

Lee went to where the two horses were tied and grabbed the lasso from the nearest saddle. In a couple of minutes the cattleman was hogtied as tight as a bank vault's door.

"Might as well shoot me now," the man grunted. "When Atticus gets back . . ."

"That's your problem," Lee answered. "You run with bloodthirsty animals, you become part of the pack." She turned away. "Bessie, grab a horse and follow me. I'm going to get Slick."

Lee hurried into the brush and followed the crushed grass and hoofprints left by the outlaws to the rope corral. Slick stood grazing at one end of the enclosure. Lee's saddle had been tossed carelessly to one side, but Slick's

160

bridle was still on his head. She quickly worked the buckles on the hobbles and then fetched her saddle and blanket. Then she worked her cinches and swung into the saddle.

"Are those two dead, Lee?" Bessie asked, her voice that of a frightened child.

"I'm afraid so, honey," Lee answered. "As dead as I could make them. C'mon—let's ride."

9

The marshall's office might just as well have been a steel cage to Monte Krupp. The heels of his boots clipped the wooden floor like the impacts of a hammer as he strode around the periphery of the room.

"We should have shot everything that moved in that hellhole and then burned it to the ground, Ben! Then we should have gone on to the Running Nine and the Double D and the other camps and leveled them too!"

Ben looked at his friend. "I know how you—"

"No, you don't know how I feel! That's half the problem. You're more concerned about this town than you are about Bessie! If it was Lee being held by those herders, there'd be bodies all over the prairie by now." Monte's voice dropped, and so did his volume. "I'll tell you this—if anyone has put a hand on Bessie or hurt her in any way, I'll treat them just like I'd treat a rattlesnake ready to strike—with a bullet."

Ben met his friend's eyes. "Monte . . ."

The drumming of a horse at a hard gallop caught the attention of both men. The pounding of hooves stopped just outside, and then the door slammed open. Carlos, red-faced and wild-eyed, yelled, "Lee ees missing!" followed by a string of Spanish words.

Ben was on his feet and away from his desk. "Carlos—English! Please! We can't follow you."

"Lee," Carlos panted. "She no come home—she ees gone. She no at Mike O'Keefe's or Missy Joplin's, she no at where they deeg the trench—she ees gone!"

Ben grabbed Carlos's shoulders. "Calm down," he demanded. "Tell us what happened. What do you mean she's gone? She left after the diggin' got started yesterday. There were hours of daylight left, and she had her rifle on her saddle."

"Come on," Monte said, easing between the two men. "Sit down for a minute, Carlos—catch your breath. Think for a bit and then tell us just what happened." He took Carlos's arm and led him as a mother leads a child, to the chair behind Ben's desk. "Sit for a moment. And then tell us."

Carlos dropped into the chair and lowered his face into his hands, drawing deep breaths. "*Sí,*" he mumbled. "But then we mus' ride. Lee, she need me thees moment . . ." He took another long breath. When he dropped his hands from his face, there were tears flowing from his eyes. He let them course down his cheeks, unashamed.

When he spoke his voice was calmer but threatening to break on each word. "She din't come back after church. We know about Monte's plan and the trench, an' I stayed at the Thumb, helpin' load the wagons with the straw an' hay and barrels of kerosene. As soon as Lee gets back, I was gonna go an' deeg with some of my men. Then Lee, she don' come."

"She hasn't been home all night, then?" Monte asked.

"No. Maria say maybe Lee stay with Missy Joplin or with Mike, so to help with digging. When day come an' no Lee, I ride to town an' check. No Ben, no Monte, no Lee. Mr. Scott, he say you gone to talk with longhorn men. I go back out an' search for Lee, thinkin' maybe Slick, he fall or something, bust a leg, maybe hurt Lee, no? I ride all morning like a *loco* man, shouting an' calling, an' see nothing. When noon come, I come back here."

A clatter from across the office snapped Monte's and Carlos's heads toward the noise. Ben was jamming shotgun shells into the pockets of his vest, and in his rush, he had dropped a handful.

Monte watched Ben for a moment. "Better get out your Sharps, Ben. And let's take your other rifles too. Carlos—how are you armed? You carrying a long gun on your horse?"

"*Sí.* An' thees." He patted the Colt holstered at his side.

"Plenty of ammunition?"

"Not so much. Lee, she don' like to keep much bullets aroun' the Thumb. She theenk that . . ."

"I think what, Carlos? That ammunition is too expensive?"

Lee walked through the open office door, followed by Bessie. Both women were haggard and sweaty, and their hair looked like they'd been attacked by a flock of crows. Bessie's face was swollen, and the puffiness around her eyes was a yellow-purple. Her work shirt and culottes were stained with dirt and blood. Lee's long skirt was ripped and her blouse untucked. Trail dirt stuck to her face.

Ben was sure the three of them had never seen such beautiful women in their entire lives.

The small office was suddenly filled with joyous voices and kissing and hugging and rapid-fire Spanish.

When things quieted down a bit, Bessie took Monte's hand. "I promised my father I'd be right back—with you," she said. "We stopped to see him first, then came here. He made me promise we'd be back in five minutes or he'd come looking for us. He . . . " The joy drained from Bessie's bruised face. She turned to Monte and buried her face in his shoulder. "Oh, Monte—Mike looks terrible. He's . . ."

"He's had a real hard time, Bessie," Ben said. "He'll be fine, now that you're safe. Go on—you two go to him. And don't forget to have Doc check you over."

Monte met Ben's eyes. "I'll be back. I'll ask you to deputize me then."

Ben nodded. "We'll talk. Go on to Mike's."

When the couple left the marshall's office, the room was suddenly quiet. Carlos, Lee, and Ben remained standing for a moment. "Let's sit down," Ben said. "You need to tell me what happened, Lee."

He moved to the chair behind his desk. Lee sat in the chair in front of the desk, and Carlos pulled another chair from against the wall, inadvertently stepping on one of the shotgun shells Ben had dropped a few moments ago. He picked it up and tossed it to Ben.

"I say thees first, before we talk, no?" Carlos said, sitting down. He turned a bit to face Lee. "Sometimes we argue, Lee. We argue 'bout horses, we argue 'bout when the hay should be cut, we argue 'bout many things. You mus' know thees: My Maria an' me, we love you like you

166

wass our blood—our family. Jus' las' week you tell me I have a head like a peeg, but I—"

Lee smiled. "I said you were pigheaded, not that you had a head like a pig."

"Same thing. But even then, I love you."

Lee's eyes were swimming with tears. "And I love you and Maria, *mi amigo*. More than I can tell you. We *are* a family."

"Ees true. An' no man can be allowed to carry you off from us like these herders done, Lee. I can no allow that." He shifted his gaze to Ben. "Ben Flood, he cannot allow that either. I mus' stay here with Ben an' Monte till thees ees over."

Lee glanced at Ben. He acknowledged what Carlos had said with a slight incline of his chin. "They need to be stopped," he said.

A long silence followed.

"I killed two of them," Lee finally said, very quietly.

Ben caught his gasp before it could escape. The word *killed* was so out of place, so terribly out of character, when coming from Lee's lips.

"Tell us about what happened. Right from the start," he said.

It wasn't a long story. Carlos and Ben sat motionless, listening to Lee's words. She ended with, "I took the lives of two men this morning. I'll have to live with that for the rest of my life."

"They were no men," Carlos said. "They were crazed *animales* that—"

"No," Lee said quietly but firmly. "They were men whose lives I ended. Killing goes against everything I believe in and stand for, and I need time to think about everything that happened."

167

"Yeah, you do, Lee," Ben said. "No doubt about that." He paused. "Look, I'm not a scholar, but didn't we read in Scripture 'bout kidnapping being punishable by death? You raised your weapon in defense of a dear friend—and in defense of yourself. It's a terrible thing to face—ending lives in war. But that's what this is: war between the forces of good and forces that have proved themselves evil."

Lee offered a half smile. "Like I said, I have lots of thinking to do. All of my life I've been taught that violence and bloodshed are wrong, that they bring pain to the Lord, that killing goes against what Jesus wants for us as we live on earth."

"Please do think on it, Lee—and pray about it," Ben said gently. "Taking lives is a terrible thing and you'll never forget that moment, but I really believe that you did nothing wrong in the eyes of the Lord."

"I wish I could believe that right now," Lee said, her voice barely audible.

Carlos stood. "You weel go home now, to Maria, no? Donny an' Vince are at the mercantile. They weel ride back with you."

"I don't need them to—" Lee began and then stopped. "Good," she said. "Thank you."

Mr. Scott removed a clean linen handkerchief from the pocket of his new denim pants and wiped his forehead. The solid thunk of pickaxes slamming into soil and the almost melodic clink of shovel blades against rocks echoed around the men at work. The trench looked as if giant hands had torn the earth, leaving a ripped seam a yard wide and four feet deep all the way around the town. Barrels of kerosene stood every twenty yards or so along the trench. Men were forking straw from farm wagons into the ditch, and young boys and girls were tramping it down.

"There you have it, gentlemen," Mr. Scott said. "The town has done a grand job."

"So have you, Mr. Scott," Ben said. "We all appreciate you ramrodding this operation."

"This thing would be half done by now—at best—if you hadn't been here, sir," Monte said. "I hope we don't have to use it, but if we do, it'll work."

"One more thing we ask of you, Mr. Scott," Carlos said.

"Oh?"

"Yeah," Ben said. "We need a couple of cases of dynamite. I don't have the cash right now, but I'll send your bill over the wire today."

"This is to assist you in moving the herders?" Mr. Scott asked.

"Yessir. It is."

"Then there will be no bill. I'll have the dynamite delivered to your office within the hour. Use it carefully and use it well, gentlemen."

The three men turned their horses into the enclosure behind Ben's office, loosening the cinches but leaving the mounts saddled. On the other side of the enclosure a scruffy-looking mule stood between the traces of a small flatbed. Two wooden cases of dynamite rested on the flatbed, along with a piece of equipment that was covered by a tarp. A Busted Thumb ranch hand sat in the driver's seat, reading a dime novel. A flashy Appaloosa was tied to the rear of the cart, appearing to be half asleep.

Monte shook his head and laughed. "I would never have thought of it, Carlos—I'll admit that to you."

169

"If it works the way you say . . ." Ben said.

"No if, *mis amigos*. She weel work jus' fine. Thees I know. I try her out five, maybe six times. The only problem ees using Maria's bes' pot—the one she order from the Monkey Ward catalog."

"Carlos's word is good enough for me," Monte said. "Let's get some coffee."

Carlos called out to the fellow with the novel. "Lenny, you can go on back to the Thumb now. Your spotted horse, he weel make the trip?"

Lenny smiled. "Oh, I think he'll make it okay, seein' that he's maybe three times as fast as that crowbait you ride."

"Lenny," Carlos said, "one day we run together, no? My fine horse Happy an' your spotted horse?"

"Count on it," the cowboy answered, untying his horse. He mounted, waved, and gigged the Appy into a lope.

"Nice movement, real good legs," Ben commented as he watched Lenny ride off.

"Those spots look good on him," Monte added.

"Bah!" Carlos exclaimed. "Fancy color don' win no race."

Inside the office, Monte started the fire in the potbelly and added coffee to the pot from a sack of Arbuckle's Extra-Grade Premium.

Ben opened the rifle case and from its very rear removed a long, deerskin-wrapped object. He untied the thongs at the top and the bottom and let the hide fall away. The stock of the Sharps rifle gleamed like the finish on a fine piece of furniture. The metal parts—the lever, the thick octagonal barrel, the trigger and trigger guard, and both side plates—glistened with light gun oil. Ben took a cloth from the rifle case and began wiping away the lubrication.

Monte watched as Ben tossed the cloth back into the rifle cabinet and worked the lever action of the big rifle. The sound was a bit harsh—like that of large gears meeting—but there was a solidity to it too, like the closing of a bank vault.

"When did you last use it?" Monte asked.

"I fire a dozen rounds or so every couple of months. I've still got my eye."

"Good. Coffee's ready."

The men sat around Ben's desk, blowing over their steaming coffee and then sipping it.

Carlos glanced out the window toward the street. "The sun, she ees stuck in the sky," he commented.

"It'll be down soon enough," Monte said.

"One thing still pester me, though, Monte. Are you sure the dynamite will no set off the longhorns?"

Monte chuckled. "I'm not sure about anything about longhorn cattle. But I know this: If a thunderstorm doesn't get them running, dynamite won't either. Like I said in church, it's the lightning—and it needs to strike directly in the herd and kill a few beef—that starts a stampede. Those cattle have seen and heard a dozen thunderstorms since they left their home ranges and were brought here."

Another pot of coffee later, the sun was well into its downward slide. The town was quiet. There were a few horses tied in front of the Drovers' Inn, but the piano inside was silent.

"They know we're coming," Monte observed. "No drunks on the street, no noise, no horse races. They're sticking tight to their camps."

"Yeah. Toole must have men watchin' us, though. We won't have a big element of surprise."

"Thanks to Carlos—and Maria's pan—I think we'll give them something to think about," Monte said.

Carlos stood. "Ees time, no?"

"Yeah," Ben said. "Let's just take a moment here an' then get to it."

Ben and Monte got to their feet. All three men closed their eyes. They didn't need spoken words—their minds and their hearts were all in the same place.

Carlos left Ben and Monte in the office as they were strapping bandoliers of the heavy Sharps cartridges over their chests. Outside, the mule honked as Carlos gigged him into a trot. Monte's nicely tailored jacket sagged on both sides from the weight of the .45 caliber bullets in the pockets. Ben's pockets were full as well. "We'll give Carlos maybe a half hour," he said. "That mule has a nice trot on him."

Minutes slouched by, each one dragging its heels.

"I never thought the Deathlings would work again," Monte said.

"We're different men now, Monte. We ain't Deathlings no more." He paused. "This is a war, though. Not exactly like the other one, maybe, but it's a war."

Monte stood and extended his hand. Ben took it silently.

"It's time," Monte said.

A crackle of gunfire spooked Monte's rental horse when they were still a couple miles from the Long Snake encampment.

"Well," Ben said. "Let's get started."

They jacked their mounts into a fast lope for a mile. The cattle on the periphery of the herd were a couple of hundred yards from the camp itself. As Ben and Monte topped a long rise that looked down on the camp, the main campfire became visible. A few other smaller fires were winking out near the wagons and the rope corral that held the string of horses. Men moved about with buckets of water, dousing their cook fires. Three men on horseback rode into the camp hard, dragging their mounts to a halt near the corral.

"See you in a bit, Monte," Ben said.

Monte swung his horse to his left; Ben turned Snorty to the right.

Ben dismounted after jogging his horse for a pair of minutes. He ground tied Snorty down on the rise, pulled the Sharps from the saddle scabbard, and walked back to the edge of the hill. He shrugged out of the bandoliers and arranged them one on each side. He drew his Colt and placed it within easy reach of his right hand. Another Colt, a backup weapon from his saddlebag, he set in the grass next to the first. He stretched out full length, his legs a foot apart, and dug his elbows into the dirt. He jacked a round into the chamber of his buffalo rifle, easing the stock against his shoulder.

Some muzzle flashes from the camp seemed to be directed at the apex of the triangle he, Carlos, and Monte had created. Carlos, at the point with the little cart, didn't return fire.

Ben fired the Sharps into the air, worked the lever, and fired again. The percussive boom of the weapon made the pistol and rifle reports from the camp sound like penny firecrackers.

For an eternity, nothing happened. Then a thin line of sparkling white light arced upward from Carlos's position and sailed smoothly toward the main campfire.

The stick of dynamite exploded with a *whomph*. A jagged ball of fire detonated fifty feet over the cowboys' heads. The horses spooked immediately, for the first few moments galloping around the edges within the rope enclosure and then taking down the rope and breaking up. The horses headed in all directions, squealing as they ran from the attack from the sky. Frenzied rifle and pistol fire rattled from the camp; the muzzle flashes looked like lightning bugs on a still summer night.

The cattle shifted restively, snorting, drawing closer together defensively, more concerned about the frantic flight of the horses than the assault from the sky—that to their dim brains was simply another storm.

Carlos twisted the fuses of two sticks of dynamite together and wedged them securely into Maria's pot, which was wired to a 6-foot-long, 2-by-4-inch beam of creosoted wood. He scratched a lucifer on the wheel of the wagon and then used his weight and muscles to force the beam downward against the heavy stagecoach spiral spring mounted on the base of the catapult. Sparks leaped from the hissing fuse, and sweat popped from Carlos's forehead as he grunted against the spring.

When he stepped back, the power of the cold steel was unleashed, and the beam whistled forward, launching the twin sticks of explosives. Carlos watched the arc of spitting light as it rose and then began its descent. A volcanic geyser of dirt, rock, and scrub grass erupted fifty feet beyond the chuck wagon. Almost immediately, the canvas of the wagon burst into flame.

Ben picked his targets carefully and fired rapid but unhurried rounds into the camp. The hubs of a stock wagon exploded one after the other, destroying the thick wooden spokes of the wheels. The wagon teetered like a wounded beast for a second and then collapsed on its side. A lantern that had been burning on the open tailgate smashed when it struck the ground. And then the canvas of that wagon, like the other, was a sheet of hungry flames.

Monte put two quick rounds into the midst of the main campfire, hurling white-hot embers, lengths of burning wood, and a screen of scarlet embers into the air. Screams, yells, and curses sounded for a few moments, but then the horrific explosions of dynamite and the deep, thudding reports of the Sharps rifles overcame all sound but their own.

Saddled and unsaddled horses raced through the chaotic camp, taking down men in their paths like battering rams. Monte's eyes picked out the dark image of a barrel in the wave of light from the burning chuck wagon. He put a slug into its center and worked the lever to fire at it again. But he didn't have to. The three-quarters-full barrel of kerosene detonated in a bolt of heat and shimmering light. The concussion slammed herders to the ground with its terrific force, and twisted pieces of shrapnel moaned through the air.

Ben fired like a well-tuned machine, aiming, squeezing the trigger, working the lever of his Sharps. The barrel of the weapon was radiating heat now, warming even the wooden stock. He stopped as he reloaded and dripped a spot of saliva on the side plate of the weapon. The moisture sizzled. He set the Sharps carefully on the ground and picked up a Colt .45.

Monte dragged his horse to a sliding stop behind Ben's stand. "We're done here—let's move up and give Carlos some cover!"

Ben grabbed the bandolier that still had a few rounds in its loops, holstered his Colt, and snatched up his backup pistol. Monte fired once as Ben ran to Snorty, and then both men rode hard to the point of their battle triangle—Carlos's position.

Carlos's face was speckled with small burns from the fuses of the sticks of dynamite. His shirt was plastered to his back and chest with sweat, and his eyes—even in the faint moonlight—were red.

"You did great, Carlos," Monte shouted. "Go on—get out of here!"

"*Una mas,*" Carlos said with a grin, twisting the fuses of five sticks together. He touched the mated strands with a lucifer and groaned as he powered the beam downward, compressing the spring. When he stepped away, the wood cried out as if in pain, but it hefted the dynamite high into the air. The three men watched its sparkling trip through the dark. The fire touched the dynamite when it was but a few yards off the ground, to the left of the flaming chuck wagon.

Ben thought it was a beautiful thing, in a sense, if one could discount the destruction and pain the dynamite caused. There was a moment when it seemed as if the entire prairie was bathed in red and yellow light, benevolent and kind. But that scintilla of time was gone, and the evil bellow of the explosives tore the fragmented camp apart.

Carlos climbed into the driver's seat and slapped the reins against the mule's back. The animal was more than ready to leave the battleground—he surged ahead like a racehorse at the sound of the starting gun.

Shouts, strings of profanity, and some loud, chilling moans of pain reached Ben and Monte as they sat on their horses, giving Carlos and the mule adequate lead time in case the herders decided to give chase.

The Long Snake camp was a burning disaster—an ugly mass of charred wagons, burning canvas and wood, and scattered supplies, clothing, and drover's equipment. A ruptured sack of flour had been flung by the force of one of the first sticks of dynamite, and the men staggering about looked like circus clowns, the white powder sticking to their sweaty faces. They'd given up hauling water from the few small water holes that allowed the herd to drink. The distance was too far and the buckets too few to have any real effect on the conflagration.

Atticus Toole stood alone, twenty yards out from his camp. He took a cigar from his pocket, saw that it was broken, and tossed it to the ground. Twenty minutes passed, and perhaps a few more, as he swept the smoking ruins with his eyes. Finally, he drew his Colt and fired six rapid shots into the air over his head. All heads swung his way. He motioned the men toward him.

The few men who dared to meet Toole's eyes looked away immediately. When he began to speak, his voice was a low growl. He paced as he spoke, taking short, clipped steps, stopping to glare wordlessly for long moments at the crowd of men and then continuing.

"This camp is done. We should've been ready for an attack, and we weren't. We can't do nothin' about that now. But I'll tell you men this: Our herds ain't goin' nowhere unless they go right on over our dead bodies. This is a war now. We were attacked, an' we're gonna counterattack—tomorrow night."

He glared at the men for a moment before going on. "I want those of you who can find your horses to ride to the other camps an' bring the ramrods and cowhands

177

back here by tomorrow midday. I don't want to hear excuses. I want all of them here, ready to go to battle. Make that real clear."

He reached into an empty vest pocket for a cigar, cursed, and glared out at the men again. "Like I said, this is a war. Between us an' the other herders, we got an army. What that army is gonna do is take over the town of Burnt Rock, an' there ain't no one to move us till we can ship our beef. The army don't care nothin' about range wars like this, and neither does Texas law. We'll move our beef in closer. Those in town who don't bother us get to live. The others we kill."

"What about the marshall an' the buffalo hunter?" one of the braver men dared to ask.

Toole was silent for a moment. "Them two and the Mex and their women are gonna do some time in jail— all of 'em in the same cell, for as long as we stick around. Anybody in town who wants to see who's in control in Burnt Rock can go an' gawk at them. Maybe bring 'em some food an' water too, 'cause we ain't about to."

10

The wind out on the prairie was warm and frolicsome, catching and hurling tumbleweeds and then dropping them like a child suddenly tired of a toy. Dust devils whirled about before the wind lost interest and let them drift back to the ground.

"Smells a bit like rain," Monte commented. "Sky's roily off to the north and east." He edged his horse closer to Ben.

"Could rain some," Ben allowed. "It's been a while. Doesn't seem like we're losin' much straw or hay, though. Packin' it down with tampers was a good idea."

The trench stretched out and around the town like a scruffy necklace, and the soil that had been excavated was now dry and crumbling and carried off by the wind. The kerosene barrels stood like lonely sentries waiting for an attack.

"Town's awful quiet," Monte said.

"Everyone's scared. Some of the people think we were a little hasty last night at the Long Snake. Even Doc was sayin' that what we did was goad 'em—give 'em a good reason to attack the town."

Monte sighed. "We had no options. If we'd let it go after they kidnapped Bessie and Lee, we might just as well have handed the town over to them right then."

"I don't know about that." Ben shook his head. "They're gonna come now, though. Sure as the sun sets at night."

"Yeah. They are—tonight, if I read them right. That Toole isn't about to let last night get by even for twenty-four hours."

The two men watched the patterns of the wind for a moment in silence.

"I see Lee is in town," Monte said. "I saw Slick tied up in front of the café."

"Yeah. She's stayin' with Bessie an' Mike for a couple of days. And Carlos and ten or so of their men rode in this mornin' too. I'm gonna have those boys up on rooftops with rifles tonight." He checked the sky. "Gonna be dark soon."

"Something tells me we aren't going to get much sleep tonight, my friend," Monte said, raising his voice a bit over the wind.

Lee poured coffee into Bessie's cup, Mike's, and then her own. It was dark now, and the temperature had dropped. The wind had steadied into a low, constant moan that rattled windows and scraped the wooden sidewalks clean of dirt, scraps of paper, and cigarette and cigar butts. Lee watched out the window of Mike and Bessie's home above the café as a clump of weeds

180

the size of a calf skittered down Main Street and out into the darkness of the prairie.

"I'm going down to the stable in a bit to check on Slick," Lee said. "He doesn't much care for this wind; it makes him nervous and skittish."

"I can't say I like it a whole lot either," Mike said. "Slick ain't the only one who gets skittish. I'm thinkin' I'll walk over to the church and set up in the steeple with Mr. Scott for a couple hours. Spell him a bit. He's got the watch tonight."

"Mike, should you be out walking around?" Bessie asked. "You haven't nearly got your strength back yet. Why not stay here, and we'll get out the checkerboard?"

"Oh, hush now, Bess. Ain't nothin' wrong with me that seein' you safe didn't fix right up." He grinned. "Anyways, on the best days either of you young'uns ever had you couldn't touch me in checkers."

"We'll just see about that later then, Mike," Lee said. "Seems to me Carlos trimmed you two games in a row a few weeks back—an' I beat Carlos like ridin' horseback beats walkin' barefoot."

Mike took his jacket from a hook near the door. "You got yourself a date later on tonight, Miss Lee Morgan. Best three outta five games?"

"I get the winner," Bessie said. "And note that I don't need to brag none about my checker game. I just play and win."

"We'll see 'bout that," Mike grunted and stepped out the door. A gust of wind blew in some dust from the street as he closed the door behind him.

"It's going to be a quiet night, except for that pesky wind," Bessie said, looking at the door. She turned to Lee with a smile. "Let's talk about my wedding."

One of the drag riders—those who work behind the herd when it's moving and contain it at night from the rear—shifted in his saddle. The low, deep murmur of far-off thunder reached his ears. Toole had left him and eight other men to tend to the Long Snake beef, and the cowboy was glad to be where he was. He'd seen what a buffalo rifle could do to flesh and bone, and he didn't care to see it again—particularly if the rifle was pointed at him.

Clouds scudded past the face of the moon. To the north and east the clouds had collected into a boiling mass that was torn every so often by tongues of lightning. The cowboy fumbled for his saddlebag and took an unlabeled pint bottle from it—his second of the night. He pulled the cork with his teeth and drank, not moving his eyes from the northeast.

The bawling of the cattle increased in volume slightly. Instinct drew the animals closer together, and in the meager light of the moon, the herd appeared as a widespread dark stain on the lighter cloth of the prairie. The stain suddenly began to shrink, to draw in on itself, as the stragglers and wanderers lumbered into the security of the mass.

The cowboy shook his head. Toole had told him and the others left behind that if they strayed from their posts they were as good as dead. Still, Atticus Toole and a small army of men were riding toward Burnt Rock—directly between the herd and the town. A clap of thunder resonated more loudly. The cowboy drank again and tossed the empty bottle aside. Rain started spattering around him.

The shape of the herd changed as he watched, drawing tighter together like a bit of quicksilver attracting and consuming other bits. A bolt of lightning illuminated the prairie, and its harsh white light glistened off thousands of widely dilated bovine eyes. The cowboy's horse danced under him, and he sawed at the animal's mouth with the reins.

An unnatural hissing sound like the threat of a cottonmouth amplified a thousand times seemed to come from all directions at once. The cowboy, a man who hadn't said the Lord's name except in vain during the last twenty years, began to mouth a faintly remembered prayer he'd learned at his mother's knee. A piercingly bright light the size of a barn door rolled through the middle of the herd, flinging long, jagged prongs of searing incandescence. Then a bull toward the rear of the herd turned a scintillating shade of blue, and thousands of baseball-sized shards of the same blue began a devil's dance among the tips of the horns of the frantic cattle.

"St. Elmo's light," the cowboy screamed, but his voice was lost in the hissing.

The stampede was on.

"King me," Mike said across the table from Lee.

Lee grimaced as she placed a checker on top of Mike's. "Of all the luck," she grumbled. "That last move of yours takes the cake, Mike."

"Luck?" Mike said, smiling broadly. "There's no luck involved. It's pure intelligence and skill." He jumped Lee's piece, darted his checker to the left, jumped another, and with a loud laugh, jumped Lee's unprotected king. "Game!" he gloated.

"Two games each, Dad," Bessie said. "The next one is the one that counts."

"Right," Lee agreed. "I was just getting the lay of the land in those games. C'mon, Mike, set 'em up!" She reached for her coffee cup next to the checkerboard, took a drink, and set the cup back down. "Did Ben say how long he was going to stay up in the steeple with Mr. Scott?" she asked. "I was hoping he might stop here to visit."

"Not much chance of that," Mike said. "He's worried about Toole an' the others comin' to town, and he figured this thunderstorm might give them some cover. Monte ain't gonna make it tonight either. He's up on the roof of the mercantile."

"Maybe those cattlemen are whipped," Lee said. "I wouldn't be surprised if come tomorrow, we saw all of them heading out." She reached for her coffee again. The cup trembled slightly on the surface of the table. "What in the world . . . ?"

The checkers began to dance on the board, jumping an inch above the board's surface and clattering to the table. The lamp above them swung in a jerky arc, its flickering light casting strange, sharp-edged shadows.

"It's the cattle!" Bessie gasped. She opened her mouth to say more, but whatever she said was smothered by the heavy tolling of the church bell. Its tones fought and conquered the persistent drumming of the rain and the howling of the wind.

Lee sprang to her feet and raced to the door. "I'm going to the church," she shouted just as thunder crashed over Burnt Rock. Mike reached out to stop her, but she was already out the door.

With sheets of rain lashing at her, she stumbled down the street toward the church. She fought to keep her balance against the wind, but her boots kept sticking in the thick slop on Main Street. The mud under her feet quivered crazily, and water leapt out of puddles. Across the street, the latticework of the telegraph office cracked free and spun away with the wind.

When she reached the church, Lee was as wet as she would have been had she swum a wide river. Her lungs burning, she dashed up the stairs to the steeple. When she burst into the tiny room directly below the bell, a fork of lightning showed her a quick daguerreotype of Ben standing at the railing with his Sharps rifle at his shoulder.

Mr. Scott was yanking the bell rope frantically, sweat glistening on his face, his movements clumsy but effective. Lee moved next to Ben at the railing.

She had a good view of the town from up there, and she could see small clusters of men wrestling with barrels of kerosene and pouring the contents into the ditch. A figure ran from behind the mercantile with a torch, and before the rain could extinguish it or the wind could tear it away, the man tossed it into the ditch. Tiny, insignificant flames sprouted where the torch landed. Another man ran out with a torch—and another.

And then it was as if fire was breaking up through the crust of the earth. The line of flame raced along the trench, the first blaze scrambling ten feet into the air, ignoring the rain, the night, the wind.

A bolt of chain lightning speared the earth, and again the prairie was illuminated. A mile out of town, a ragged line of cowboys were running for their lives in front of a great mass of panicked longhorn cattle. Eerie handfuls of blue light leaped about from horn to horn and animal to animal, whipping them on.

One of the horsemen went down in a crash that threw him and his horse into a grotesque somersault of arms and legs and saddle. In a matter of seconds the herd was upon them. The unstoppable mass of living creatures didn't even slow as they overran the doomed horse and man.

Lee put her hand to her mouth and tried to pry her eyes away from the scene. But she couldn't.

The men were pushing their horses too hard, asking too much of them on the slick, flooded prairie. Another went down. A horse swerved into another at its side, and a pair of riders slammed into the resulting carnage. And the herd went on.

Ben lowered his rifle, his face a pasty white. "Those cowboys ain't gonna make it—none of 'em are gonna make it!"

Lee clutched his arm with both her hands, and they stood transfixed and helpless as the blanket of moving death surged over the dozens of men and their exhausted horses.

The cattle ran on, a tidal wave of flesh and bone and fear and death. As the herd approached the town, instinct triumphed over sheer panic. The trench fire was blazing well as the wind whipped the flames higher, and something told the cattle that the known evil from which they ran was lesser than the frightening new threat of licking, grasping fire.

Ponderously, like the Red Sea parting, the wave of cattle cut in two as the animals swung to either side of the fulminating ditch.

It took the better part of twenty minutes for the herd to pass. Then stragglers, the old and the sick and the injured longhorns, limped along or lumbered past as best they could in the wake of their peers. Their distraught bawling was a heartrending sound.

Lee moved in front of Ben and hugged him close to herself, her face against his chest. His arms went around her tightly enough to squeeze most of her breath away. "All those men," she said, "all those men caught in front of the stampede."

"They were comin' to attack the town, Lee," Ben said gently. "I don't think Monte and Carlos and I could've held them off for long, even with the help of your men. And after Toole put us down, there's no tellin' what would've happened to Burnt Rock and to you and Bessie." He breathed deeply and exhaled. "Still, it's a hideous way to end a life—tryin' to outrun a stampede in the middle of a thunderstorm with that lightning flashin' and the thunder rattlin' everything . . ." He eased out of Lee's arms, and together they started down the stairs.

They stopped at the bottom. "Ben," Lee said, "that man who abducted me said that you and Monte were called Deathlings during the war."

Ben lowered his eyes. "I'd have told you about it eventually, Lee. It's . . . a real confused bunch of memories about the worst years of my life. It was a time of blood and pain and, well . . ."

"No, Ben—wait. I want to say this: You needn't worry any longer how or when you're going to tell me. You've never spoken much about the war, and that's fine. I don't need to know, and I don't even want to know. The man I met and fell in love with is a different man than the one who fought in the War Between the States."

She took his hand and led him outside. The smoke from the trench seemed thicker than it had in the steeple, hugging the ground like fog. But the rain and storm had passed along with the stampede. Long sections of darkness broke the chain of the trench where the fires had died after consuming the fuel that had fed them.

Monte and Bessie stood behind the mercantile, looking out into the prairie with their arms around one another's waists. Monte turned at the sound of Ben's

187

boots. His face was grimy and there were burn marks on his jacket and sleeves, but his smile stood out like a beacon on a stormy night.

"You got a decent suit of clothes to wear when you're our best man, Ben?" Monte asked.

"If I don't, I'll buy one. The thing is, well, you've never been a man to waste time or money, have you?"

Lee felt the slightest bit of moisture from Ben's palm as he held her hand. When he spoke, there was a tremble in his voice.

Monte looked confused. "I suppose that's true enough."

Ben cleared his throat. "Seems to me that maybe a pair of marriages at the same time might work out jus' fine—one big reception after the service. See what I mean?"

"Oh, Ben!" Lee gasped.

"I'm gonna send a wire out tonight resignin' my post here as marshall. Soon as a new man is on the job, I'm gonna put my weapons away an' hope an' pray I never have to use them again."

Lee hardly knew what to do. She couldn't even look Ben in the eye.

But Ben turned her toward him. "'Course, this all kinda depends on whether Miss Lee Morgan will have me as a husband." There was no tremble in his voice now. "Lee? Will you marry me?"

Lee took hold of his other hand. "You know that I will. But . . . I want to hear myself say it—yes, Ben, I will marry you."

She barely heard the little cheer that erupted from Monte and Bessie. She was looking too deeply into Ben's eyes.

Author's Note

Although this book is a work of fiction, ball lightning and St. Elmo's fire are very real natural phenomena, and both were responsible for many stampedes in the cattle-driving years of the American West. In the worlds of science and meteorology, St. Elmo's fire is stated to be a super-heated ionized gas that forms around the tips of raised, pointed conductors, including the horns of cattle. Christopher Columbus encountered and wrote about St. Elmo's fire on his second voyage, and Magellan kept records about it during his circumnavigation of the globe. Both men's ships had been touched by the rare occurrence. Many people believe that the Hindenburg zeppelin disaster in 1937 was caused by St. Elmo's fire. Also referred to in contemporary times as "corona discharge," it continues to be seen and reported throughout the world.

Ball lightning, a more familiar and much less rare phenomenon, is the initial highly charged electrical disturbance that generates the detached bolts of strangely glowing blue light when it deconstructs after touching down on earth or bodies of water.

Paul Bagdon, a lifelong horseman and former rodeo competitor, reflects his keen understanding of the horse/rider relationship in his writings. Twenty-seven of his action-adventure novels have been published in the general market, and he is the author of 250 short stories and articles. Bagdon is currently an instructor for Writer's Digest School and lives in Rochester, New York.